Onion John

Onion John

JOSEPH KRUMGOLD

Illustrated by Symeon Shimin

HarperTrophy
A Division of HarperCollinsPublishers

Library of Congress Catalog Card Number: 59-11395
ISBN 0-690-59957-9
ISBN 0-690-04698-7 (lib. bdg.)
ISBN 0-06-440144-8 (pbk.)

First Harper Trophy edition, 1984.

For
my wife
HELEN

Chapter 1

Up until I turned twelve years old the kind of friends I had were what you'd expect. They were my own age more or less. Most of them were born here in Serenity along with me. And all of us went to the same school together.

As long as those were the friends I had, nothing too serious ever happened to any of us, except a broken arm now and then or six stitches in somebody's scalp or scarlet fever. The worst was when we were six years old and Eechee Ries had to be pulled out of the pond behind the closed down piano factory. Eech had to get worked over with a Pulmotor. They had him breathing again in about ten minutes and he came out fine. That was the worst. Until I got to know Onion John and we two came to be the best of friends.

Onion John was a lot different from anyone I ever hung out with before. Like his age. No one actually knew how old he'd be. But considering he was six feet and three inches tall with a mustache, it was a good guess that Onion

John was well along in years. Anyway, he was a lot older than I am.

He used to live up on Hessian Hill, Onion John did, in a house he built out of piled up stone and four bathtubs and no running water. Once a month he'd get up in the middle of the night, according to the way the moon was, to cook up a stew with chunks of lead in it and maybe some chipped stone he collected and half a rabbit sometimes and always a little wood alcohol to make a blue flame. It wasn't a stew for eating. It was to get gold out of the moon, to make his fortune.

I never saw any fortune come out of what Onion John was cooking. And now I guess I never will. Because everything's changed for Onion John, on account of us getting to be friends the way we did.

It happened the day we played Rockton Township for the Little League Pennant. Onion John didn't come out to watch the ball game, actually. He came to go shopping in the garbage dump behind center field which is the position that I play. The Serenity dump for John was the same as the supermarket is for most people. He went there for whatever he needed. And if he didn't find what he was looking for he usually came across something he could use just as well. So the sight of Onion John out there on the garbage dump, that day, there was nothing too different in that.

Except everything else about the afternoon was so different I took special notice, more than ever before, of

Onion John. It was the biggest ball game I ever played in. And the most important ball player on the Serenity team was me. Not that I'm the best one. There's George Connors who bats fourth, he's the best slugger our age with this trick, he has, of twisting his wrists when he steps into a ball. Ries, who almost drowned that time, he's our best pitcher. And in the field, Bo Hemmendinger is the handiest.

I'm lucky. The only way I ever managed to stay on the team was because of all the luck I had. The part I liked about the Little League was the bus rides we took when we played away from home, the singing, and what happened every afternoon just batting it around at practice. The most I ever looked for out of a ball game was not to get noticed, particularly.

Yet I was the one the whole championship depended on. According to Mr. Miller who was the editor of the only newspaper we have in town, the *Lamp*.

I'd just come into the hardware store to bring my father his cooked lunch, the way I'd been doing all that summer, and while the bell on top was still jingling, I heard, "Congratulations, Andy. You're in the news."

It was dark inside the store with all the shades pulled down, especially after the glitter the sun made outside. When I made him out, I saw my father over in kitchenware waiting on Mrs. Kinnoy. "It's on the desk! Take a look at yourself."

Across the front page of the *Lamp* was this headline

about us. LITTLE LEAGUERS MEET ROCKTON LIONS IN PENNANT TILT. When I saw the picture of the ball team underneath the headline, I asked my father, "Who am I? Which one?"

The sort of picture it was you could make out Mr. Donahue on one side. He runs the barber shop down at the bridge and he coaches us. And on the other side you could make out my father. He's the president of the Rotary Club and they collected to buy us our bats and gloves and things. They were tall.

But in between, all you could see was twelve uniforms all in a row with hardly any faces to them because of the way things were smudged. We all looked the same, Burke, Hemmendinger, Ries, Schwarz, Connors, Maibee and Berry, like a bunch of dark shadows standing in the fog with the word SERENITY across our chest.

This is the special way that the *Lamp* prints a lot of its pictures and I never minded it before. Most of the time I know what the picture is supposed to look like anyway, whether it's the Episcopal Church, or the firehouse, or construction starts on the new $125,000 school. Except this time I'd just as soon not have to suppose, seeing it was my first picture in the paper.

"Who are you?" my father turned around to answer me. "Why don't you look underneath." Below the picture were all our names from left to right and the fifth was *Andrew J. Rusch, Jr.* I counted out to the fifth blur and it didn't look familiar. I folded the paper under my arm and went over to where my father was shaking his head at the two fingers Mrs. Kinnoy held up. "No laundry faucet ever took a washer that size," he told her.

In a hardware store you go crazy with sizes. You take washers, they go from an eensy quarter inch right up to two and a half, even three inches for a valve in a water main. If someone comes in without a worn washer or without the faucet itself to get fitted, you're licked. Unless you use the kind of a system my father has.

He led the way to the back wall where we keep pipe samples and fittings and he told Mrs. Kinnoy to pick out the faucet back there that looked like the one she had at home. He left her with one finger to her lips and he turned to me.

"How'd you like it?" He took the paper for another look.

"There don't seem much use to a picture, if all you can recognize is your name."

"This is it." Mrs. Kinnoy turned from the shelf with a faucet in her hand. "Rimco. That's even the trademark. What's wrong?" she asked when she looked at me.

She examined the paper with my father and it reminded Mrs. Kinnoy of her high school graduation picture when all that came out was her sash. "What a shame!" she said. "Why don't you call Ernie Miller and let him hear how you feel, Andy. Just tell him."

"I feel all right."

"That's no way to talk." My father had his arms crossed and he held on to his elbows. "Not for some one who's going to the moon." We joked about me going to the moon sometimes, me and my father, because of the good marks I brought home in arithmetic. "Out in space you've got to stand on your own two feet."

He led the way across the store. "I'd like Ernie Miller to learn he can't do this! The time's come when he ought to stop mutilating the good people of this town."

He brought us to where we have an office partitioned off behind three show cases, on one side cutlery and in the front fishing items and on the third side, guns. He dialed. I was ready to hear my father let Mr. Miller have it, when he handed the phone across the counter.

"Me?"

"Go ahead. You're the one's disappointed."

I wasn't so disappointed. But my father was right. It wasn't his picture in the paper. And I couldn't stand there with the phone in my hand, all the yelling came out of it. I said, "Hello."

It wasn't a good time to talk to Mr. Miller. He told me Judge Brandstetter had just called to complain about some T's that were missing out of his name. And the whole Connors family was taking oxygen because their girl got engaged and the *Lamp* never even mentioned it. "And now you're telling me you're mutilated!" Whatever it was he pounded, it sounded like a drum. "All right, let me see you get out there and win that championship tomorrow. If you think you rate special attention from the *Lamp*, Andy, then you're the one I'm going to watch. But if you lose, well then my boy, maybe then, I'll have something to complain about."

"Me lose? How can I? There's eight others on the team."

"You're the only one who called. Now show me why you're so important!" Mr. Miller hung up.

That's how I became the most important ball player all of a sudden on the Serenity team. And not only that. Everything else about the game was what you'd never expect. The ball park was jammed with the biggest crowd we ever had, better than forty people. And when the Rockton rooters showed up, there were twenty more of those. The Lions, every one on their team had grown six inches in the two weeks since we beat them by one run. They looked bigger than I ever expected. And I never expected everyone to start talking how we should lose.

But Coach Donahue told us, "I don't care if you lose. Just let me see a lot of pepper out there."

And my father. "Losing's just a number on a scoreboard, Andy. Don't think about it. Let yourself go and have fun."

And my mother. "Baseball's a sport. It makes you healthy." Her idea was that you got just as healthy losing as you did when you won.

Maybe it was all strategy. To keep us from getting nervous. I didn't see the good of it, as strategy. It didn't keep me from getting nervous. I was afraid some of the others would follow the strategy and then we really would lose. And with Mr. Miller sitting behind first base in his white droopy straw hat, it could mean this was the last game I'd ever play for the Little League after he finished writing me up in the *Lamp*.

The only thing wasn't a surprise that afternoon was the sight of Onion John out back in the garbage dump putting together a pile of old brick. Wherever you happened to be in Serenity, Onion John was what you'd expect. He was like the street lights turning up after supper when it got dark. Or the afternoon shadows moving under the locust trees in the park across from the courthouse. He was there when you were on your way to school, or fishing for blue gill in the creek and when you ran down to the A&P for your mother. He was always around.

He was even the kind of noise you didn't pay any attention to. The whirr of a lawn mower in back of Miss Rorty's house. Or shears clicking behind Judge Brandstetter's high hedge. And he'd be one of the first things you saw in the morning when you happened to look out the window, this long overcoat moving down the street with a pair of heavy sneakers below and a knitted hat that came to a point above, and over his shoulder a burlap bag always bulging and in his other hand, a spade. Mostly I never gave John a second look.

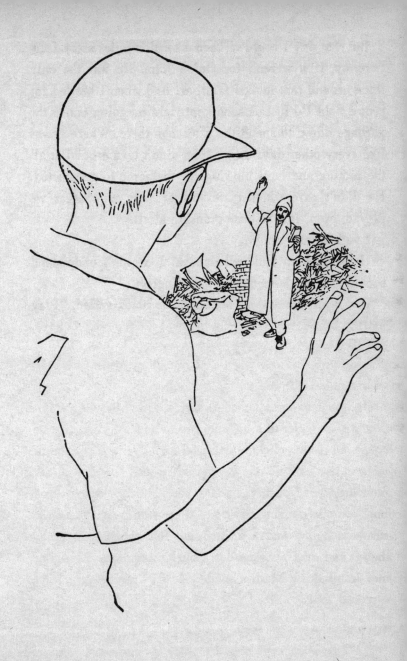

But that day I could've been a million miles away from Serenity, if it weren't for Onion John. He was the only thing around that looked familiar. And when I headed for center field I'd just as soon kept right on going out to the garbage dump to spend the afternoon there. Where it was like every other day. Onion John didn't turn around at all the rooting and horn blowing for the game to get started. He didn't care whether we lost or won or whether we played, even, for the championship at all.

I yelled hello at him.

He looked up and yelled back. I couldn't understand because Onion John doesn't talk English.

Ben Wolf, the umpire behind home plate, yelled, "Play ball!"

Chapter 2

I looked around for an old buttercup that sticks out of the ground where I usually stand. In the first game of the season I made a blind reach with my bare hand and came down with the ball, sliding on my shoulder, to find it waving underneath the peak of my hat, all yellow. Ever since it's been a lucky piece, like a four leaf clover. I hardly had time to find it before Eechee Ries let go with his first pitch. But I did and I was all set, as set as I'd ever be, when the game started.

Their first time at bat, the Rockton Lions didn't get anywhere. The lead off man struck out. The next dribbled to short. And then an easy pop up made it one, two, three. Not a ball came out of the infield. So it couldn't have been very interesting for Mr. Miller if all he was watching was me.

All he could see was the way I kept my hat tight and my belt up and my pants legs pulled down. It was inside, where everything went on. My back went into every pitch, to get a little extra into Eechee's delivery. And the muscles in my legs began to ache, helping everybody to run a little faster. I don't know what my stomach was doing but every ball that hit the catcher's mitt echoed down there. If Mr. Miller thought everything depended on me, that's the way it worked out, inside. I played every position on the team to keep those first three Lions from getting a hit.

Maybe that's why I got such a clout myself, at the first ball pitched to me, just to be able to do something on the outside. I ended up on third base with Maibee and Connors going over the plate and Serenity two whole runs ahead. We were out in front. And it was one hundred per cent pure homogenized luck. It came in way over my head, the ball did. I couldn't hold back. The bat went boom. And there I was on third.

I stood on top of the base and listened to the roar. It looked as if everybody in the stands had hiccups the way they kept pounding each other on the back. It looked like there was a change in strategy. Mr. Donahue and my father and my mother, too, they jumped and got hoarse along with everyone else, holding two fingers in the air. The big idea seemed to be we ought to go ahead and win now instead of not caring if we lose.

Bill Berry took a last strike and left me stranded on third base. I headed for my buttercup out in center field. Onion John was still going on the way you'd expect, if no one else was. He was still picking up old brick, chipping away with a hammer to loosen the cement. He had a pretty good pile built up. I thought maybe I could get him interested in baseball, now we were ahead. I shouted at him, "Two big ones for Serenity." I held up both arms. "And a big goose egg for Rockton."

Onion John let out a bellow like the game was over and we had the pennant sewed up. Only it wasn't the score. It was the brick he was working on, had him excited. He came out of the dump holding two of them up and laughing as if they were rubies. One thing about Onion John, whatever he was doing, if someone came along he was always ready to stop and talk things over.

I had to wave him back. There was a Rockton batter up at the plate. Besides I wouldn't know what he was talking about even if there was time to listen. The way John spoke was his own secret. Most of the words he used were full of x's and z's and noises like *ptchky* and *grvtch*. It was a high speed language full of jokes, from the way he carried on. Every so often, talking away, he'd get too much for himself and bust out. There was no way of telling whether the jokes were that good or not. The only part of his conversation I ever understood was the end of it. He said, "Well, good day," each word separate and clear and then you knew he was finished with whatever he was telling you.

That's what he said now when he saw that I was busy. He pulled at the point on the top of his hat and he said,

"Well, good day." I watched him go back into the dump.

With the first pitch I got my insides into the ball game, again, and my muscles. Up to now the only things Mr. Miller could write about me had to be at least good. But there were five more innings to go where anything could happen.

It was right then, on top of the second inning, when the game just about came to an end for me. There was a Lion on third. Then a walk from Ries put a Lion on first. Two on. And two out. I kicked up a chunk of dirt around the buttercup. It held up great the buttercup did, in the first inning when I got my hit. I tried to keep it working for that last out.

The Lion at bat swung. At the sound of the hit I started running. That's the way a good outfielder's supposed to work. All he has to hear is the crack of the bat and he knows where the ball's going. I swung around and I headed for a black spot right in front of the garbage dump, where it was burnt. I had a full breath and I went, straight for the deep end of center field.

"Go, man. Go, go, go." It was Eechee on the mound.

I looked over my shoulder. The ball was coming down behind me.

"Go, go, go!"

Where'd he want me to go? The ball was dropping right on the spot I started from.

"No!"

That was my father. I turned. The whole place went dead quiet, everything stopped. Even the ball seemed to hang up high where it was. The ball park was a picture in the paper. My father stood on the top of the bench, still, his finger pointed into the sky. My mother's face was hid in her hands, her elbows sticking straight at me. Mr. Miller had his white hat stretched out like he was waiting for the ball to drop into it.

The only sound was the clink of Onion John's hammer. It kept time and he started to sing a little tune. There were three deep notes and everything snapped back to life. The ball dropped as I ran and I dove for it. There was a scream. The ball went past me. A grunt from the stands came rolling out over the infield.

Everybody wanted me to do something different.

"Go, go, go!" Eechee wouldn't let up.

"Third, Andy. Get it to third."

"Here—me. Give me the toss. Me!"

"Watch it."

"Get it home."

There was no use getting it home, or doing anything much. The Rockton man was home. It was a home run with two men on base coming in ahead. Three to two. The picture was three for them, two for us, with me stretched out flat in center field.

The ball was in the dump. I don't see how anyone could know so little about baseball but Onion John figured the game was over. Maybe it was because he saw me taking it easy, just lying on the grass. Anyway he picked up the ball and brought it out to where I was with the idea, now I wasn't so busy, we could have that talk. When he saw my uniform all streaked and dirty he thought to make me feel better. Instead of giving me the ball, he reached underneath his overcoat, and then underneath a second overcoat. He wore them summer and winter. He finally got down to his pants pockets and he brought out a nickel.

I reached for the ball. John rubbed it clean in his hands and gave it to me. I gave him a smile to thank him. He settled down for a visit. He pointed to the clouds over the Munkachunk Mountains and came out with a lot of noises that, at least, cheered him up. And to tell the truth they were pretty good looking clouds at that, big thunderheads crowding up high over the hills.

"Let me have it, Andy." It was Bo Hemmendinger yelling from second base.

"I got to go now," I told Onion John.

"Well, good day," he stretched his hat off his head.

I tossed the ball to Bo and he relayed it to Ries. I went back to where I was standing and there wasn't any buttercup. The header I took scooped it out of the ground neat as a bulldozer. I kept looking for it the rest of the inning and right after Rockton was tagged for their last out, I saw it. It was laying underneath a hunk of dirt and it was starting to dry up.

16

"It's the breaks," said my father at the bench. "You can't get all the breaks, Andy. To come right down to it, that's part of the fun of the game."

I didn't know we were playing for fun again. It was confusing the way the strategy shifted back and forth. I turned around to see how Mr. Miller looked. He sat there in his white hat looking like nothing in particular. I guess he was making up his mind what to write in next Thursday's *Lamp*.

"Plenty of time left," said my father. "Three to two and there's four and a half innings to go. We're only one run behind."

"What happens," I didn't go into the buttercup part, "if you don't feel so lucky anymore?"

"You make your luck." My father pulled up my belt in back. "If you need any. It's nothing you have to count on, Andy. Not you, if you just let yourself go loose and natural. You're a natural ball player. You've got it."

My father was right.

I won the ball game. I hit a homer in the last half of the sixth with two on. And there it was, Serenity 5, Rockton 3. What's more there wasn't anything lucky about it. I knew I was going to get the home run even before it happened. I knew just the groove the ball was coming in on. I knew how I got my left foot out, and my hip, was just the right way. It was the longest ball anyone hit all afternoon. And from the way the place went to pieces, the bomb that went off, even Onion John turned around to watch. All that was left for me to do was run around the bases. And to be happy along with everybody else.

And I certainly was. Now that I was rounding first, and second and third, Mr. Miller didn't have anything to write except Serenity was champ of the Little League. He didn't have anything to print about me, unless it was how I helped to get the pennant. I didn't have to say goodbye to anybody. Not to Eech or Hemmendinger or Bitsy or George Connors. They were the ones I was going to be with for the rest of the summer, same as always.

"You see!" My father tackled me high as I came in from home plate. "That's the kind of a guy you are!" He lifted me up on the bench where I was harder to reach and got less of a pounding. "You're a winner!"

The auto horns blew with everyone getting back into their cars, five honks and then three. Five and three, all keeping time together.

"Ries's drug store!" My father stuffed us back into our windbreakers. "Flips and splits, everybody. They're all on me." He took my cap off. "What'll you have, slugger?"

"A plate of chocolate ice cream."

"That's what you always have. Go ahead, spread yourself. You've had a big day."

"Except for those four and a half innings." Hauling our bats and buckets and the rest, the mob of us walked back to where the cars were. The yelling and the horns kept up. "The only place I wanted to be most of the game was out in back there, on the garbage dump with Onion John. Especially, those innings."

"What's a couple of innings? I was sure you'd come through."

"Were you?"

"Positive." He shook the back of my neck.

"I wasn't. Not about winning. And not about pepper. Or having fun. Or getting healthy, what went on inside I wasn't even sure about that."

"There wasn't any question in my mind. I knew."

He sorted us out for the ride back to town. "Quit crowding! No more than six kids to a car."

"I think I'll hoof it," I told him.

"Get in, there's plenty of room."

"Through the dump, I'll get down to the drug store as fast as you."

"Sure, but why walk?"

"I want to see what goes on out there, with Onion John."

"John?" My father shoved Hemmendinger's backside into the car and slammed the door. "Up to you." He took the bat I was carrying out of my hand. "John won't be interested in how the game turned out."

"Even so. Now it's all over, I thought I'd walk through the dump."

It was quiet out there, with the horns finished and the crowd gone. John was glad I'd come because he was so proud to show me the pile of brick he had. It was a fine looking collection of brick. A lot of them were almost whole, with only corners broken off.

He had a lot to tell me. So I sat down on the brick and listened. None of it came across. But even so, it was nice to get out there at last. And once you took notice of Onion John, you couldn't help but be interested to watch him talk, no matter what it was he said. With his hands chopping and slicing, and his eyes so busy, and his cheeks and shoulders working, I never saw anybody get such a workout from just a conversation.

When he laughed, I got to doing it too, he was having such a good time. Then I thought I caught a couple of words.

"Cows in the sky?" I asked him. "Is that what you said?"

He stopped and his eyes went wide, looking at me. He nodded. They were right, the words I'd heard. No one else ever understood anything he said except, of course, "Well, good day."

He let me have the same mouthful over again. This time it was just noise again, none of it hung together. But the thing is, I'd done it once! That was important enough to Onion John. He stared at me like I was a magician.

He came over and we shook hands again. "Mayaglubpany!" he said. Later I found out what that meant. "Friends." And that's what we got to be, after the Rockton game, that afternoon.

Chapter 3

We put in a lot of time together the next few days, experimenting. There had to be something I did those couple of seconds out on the garbage dump that brought him in so clear. I didn't know what it was and Onion John didn't know either. But there had to be something about me that was worth looking into.

We investigated me all over town, wherever it was we happened to meet. Most of the time we put in was on the bridge on High Street. This is the coolest sight we have in Serenity, where the water comes spilling out of the mill pond back into Musconetty Creek. We don't have a mill any longer, only McSwain's Feed Store where the mill used to be. But the dam's still in great shape and you can spend hours watching the green water curl over and come up white and bubbling as it goes under the bridge. The two of us hung on a rail, thinking of different tests to make and then trying them.

Onion John would try talking slow or fast, or in little

chunks with big spaces between, or even in single words. He'd speak in a high voice or very deep, or he'd whisper. Then he'd stop and watch me, to see what'd happen. For all the smooth shining water I watched go barreling over that dam, we didn't get anywhere.

The thing is Onion John understood English, a lot of it anyway. And I could get him to repeat words, like a second grader. But that wasn't what we were after. It was the slam bang, mile a minute clatter he made, if I could get that tuned in again then Onion John would be free to say whatever he had in mind. Our problem was the same as in spying, when you're up against trying to decipher a code.

We were on Water Street one noon time. It was dead hot and I'd just come back from swimming. I met up with Onion John on the way down to the hardware store. I felt lazy. There wasn't anything moved in all the heat on Water Street except the one stop light we have in town, at the corner of High, going from red to green to red again. All there was to listen to was humming that came from the bushes and flowers in front of the houses and every so often the croak of a frog from the pond behind the piano factory. And Onion John, who never let up. We could've been the only ones in Serenity with all the quiet and the burnt up smell there was that August. Onion John went on about the smell and the terrible weather we were having, without rain, and the scandal it was.

"What kind of scandal?" I asked him.

John stopped. He almost tripped. He grabbed me by the shoulders. I looked up and got blinded with the sun. Then it hit me. I'd been listening to him for the last two minutes. I'd understood most everything he said.

We held on to each other. We tried to keep everything the way it was, quiet. We took a couple of steps and got back to walking. John didn't let out a word. Then walking together, him as tall as he was with me looking up at him every so often, he took a chance. He let go.

John told me this was the worst summer he'd ever seen in Serenity. The kind of dry spell we were having the whole world could get burnt if rain didn't come. It was a scandal the way people went around not caring, not trying to do anything about it.

I've talked about the weather all my life. But I never heard anything so amazing as that. It all came across. What John had to say about the weather was absolutely clear. We had it. I knew how to listen to Onion John. There was a way to it and I could see just the way it was. And there couldn't be any fluke to what happened. John went on about the weather and I understood him! I couldn't hold back any longer.

"Mayaglub!" I yelled, trying for that word back on the dump.

"Mayaglubpany!" he shouted to show me how it went.

We stood on the corner of High and Water Street and we let go at each other. "Mayaglubpany!"

The window over Ries's drug store opened and Eechee looked out, with a piece of bread in his hand from the lunch he was having.

"What's up?" he shouted.

"Wait'll you hear!"

"What?"

"Onion John."

I took Eech up to Hessian Hill that afternoon to listen to him. We found Onion John tying rocks in a tree. The tree grew sheepnose apples. They're a yellow kind that comes down to three rounded points like the muzzle of a sheep, if you want to think about it that way. You wouldn't want a better apple to eat, more juicy. And they're early. The first apple you have every year, usually, was out of the sack Onion John brought to town when you happened to meet him and he'd give you one.

We climbed up to help, even though neither of us had ever heard of anybody tying rocks in a tree. John had nine of them, big as softballs. His idea was that the rocks would make the apples ashamed, hanging so close by and heavy. And the apples would try hard to catch up and become big and heavy too.

It didn't seem like much of an idea to me. But then, I never did let on about the buttercup I had in center field. That was only an idea too, and how could you tell about it, whether it worked or not? Without saying what I thought, I passed on to Eech how John explained about the rocks.

"How do you know what he said?" Eech asked me. "I mean why can't I hear him."

"Getting the hang of it takes time. Listen some more."

All the time we worked in the tree, Onion John never stopped talking so Eech had plenty to listen to. When he got the last rock hung, Eech sat down in the leaves above me. "Not a word! I'd just as soon listen to a broken crank shaft, all I get out of him."

"You're not doing it right, come on down."

John dusted off a couple of places for us, with his hat, down in the crotch of the tree. When we sat down he took a couple of onions out of his overcoat pocket for us. And even though they were beauties, because he grew the best onions around, neither Eech nor I felt like one.

John ate onions the way other people ate apples or pears. And always he used his big jackknife, slicing each mouthful. Holding the slice between the blade and his thumb, he ate very slowly.

Talking away, John waved his hand along the river. From up there in the tree on Hessian Hill you could see where the river came out of the water gap and turned and flashed around into the rapids, south of town, near a new plant down there called General Magneto. John shook his fist at the clouds. They were the same kind of thunderheads as on the day of the ball game, white and piled up over the hills like a sky full of fresh dried laundry. John mooed. He ate a piece of onion and looked as if he were going to cry.

He put two fingers alongside his ears and he growled. He leaned over to me and he whispered. He laughed. And he slapped the tree.

"Is that so?" I asked John. "Why do they eat shadows?"

"Who eats shadows?" Eech lay hold of my T-shirt and pulled me around. "Where do you get shadows? I have an earache from listening so hard."

"That's the trouble. You can't listen to him that way, not too hard."

I explained to Eechee how trying to follow John so close was the mistake I made first off. It was only when I didn't pay any particular attention to him, when I didn't care so much, that I started to get the drift. I described to Eech how you had to watch Onion John and keep hearing what he said all together, without trying. "You know what it's like? Like listening to the band concert on Sunday night."

"The American Legion Band? I hear that fine."

"Well, you don't try to listen to the flute separate, do you, or the big horn or each note one after the other? You kind of take it all in together. They play 'Stars and Stripes' and you get to know what it's about just by listening to everything at once. Not each little toot. And it's the same with him, the way you have to listen to Onion John."

"Except 'Stars and Stripes' is a tune. It don't mean anything. If there was anything you had to say, like pass the butter, you could bang out 'Stars and Stripes' from here to next January. And it won't get you any butter."

"As far as that goes." I turned to Onion John who watched us, very interested, as we talked. "Would you please pass the butter?"

John lifted his shoulders to apologize he didn't have any butter. He brought out another onion to see if that would do instead.

"No thanks."

"What does that prove?" asked Eech. "Except he understands English. I know that."

"And he speaks it too. Only it's mixed up with a lot of other odds and ends, his own kind of sounds. That's why you have to listen to him in a new kind of way. Lazy, and not too close. And pretty soon all the words he's got hidden start to come out. They surprise you."

"Okay." Eech leaned back where he was sitting and stretched out and closed his eyes. "Is this lazy enough?"

"You got to watch him too. That's as important a part as all the rest."

Eech opened his eyes. "Start him up."

"The shadows?" I turned to Onion John. "Why do they eat shadows?"

John went back into high. He sailed his hands past us. He whistled. Talking fast, he gathered the air around him into big piles. He put a big bunch of air on my lap. And another big bunch on Eechee. Then he whispered again to both of us, winking. He finished with the same kind of laugh as before.

"Ever hear anything like that?" I asked Eech.

"It's just no use." Eech sat up. "It all goes by me like a fast freight. What's he talking about?"

I explained to Eech how bad John was worried about the weather. And how sore he was at the thunderheads, the way they'd been hanging over the Munkachunks day after day without doing anything. It was their fault, John said, we didn't get rain.

According to John, the thunderheads were scouts for the rest of the clouds, scattered like a herd of cows over the sky, grazing through the blue up there further than you could see. The thunderheads came on first and they'd mutter and mumble at each other to decide whether this was a good place for the others to collect. The way you see a couple of cows pick out one end of a field, sometimes. And then the others would gather along when they're quiet from eating and are full and ready to be milked.

If the thunderheads decide they like a place, they start up a wind to whistle the rest in. And from all over the sky, the clouds bunch up and flock together eating the shadows on the ground as they come. Because that's what they live on, Onion John explained. A cloud sops up shadows the way a cow eats alfalfa until the herd grows so big and full the sky is packed tight and there aren't any more shadows. All that's left is a gray day.

And once they are full up, pretty soon the rain that's in

the clouds comes spreading out, blowing across the fields, driving through the trees and running off the roof. They let out a storm. And to keep the rain coming harder and harder, the big thunderheads rumble and bellow and go charging through the herd, their horns sharp as lightning.

"You're right," Eech sat forward from his branch. "I never heard anything like that before."

"The only trouble is those thunderheads have been looking over this valley the last four or five days without doing anything. John argues we have to make up their minds for them."

"Whose minds? The clouds?"

I nodded. That was one of the reasons John was so happy I could understand him. Now I could tell everybody how to manage. The whole town had to stop eating for a day and drink only water. And then there had to be a procession. With the most important up front, the mayor, and the president of the bank, Mr. Weems, and all the ministers and school teachers leading the rest of us down to the creek. We had to carry torches and sing a special hymn. And at the end we had to toss the mayor in the creek with all his clothes on.

Eechee shook his head when I told him. "Old Man Weltershot. In the creek? Never happen in a million years."

"Everyone would certainly enjoy it, him and his big hat."

"That part, maybe. But who'd go for not eating all day?"

"I guess not." Eech and I didn't see where anyone in Serenity would go parading around with torches on the off chance it might rain. And that's what I told John. He was very disappointed. He threw away the little piece of onion he had left and snapped his jackknife shut and the next thing he said, I didn't understand at all. He went on talking to himself and it must've been in his own language. Not a word came through.

"What's he saying?"

"I don't know." I was afraid I'd lost the knack I had.

"He looks real sad."

"He's bound, that's why, on having a procession. Look Eech!" I explained the part where Onion John whispered. "He said it didn't have to be everybody in town. He says the more the better, but even a few people would do. Maybe even us, we three might work. Should I ask him?"

"For a procession that'd be sparse, only us two and John."

"We could spread out."

"I guess we could." Eech picked a leaf and twirled it. "But why? Do you think it'll do any good?"

"It'll make him happy. And it can't do any harm. And what if it works. We'll be the first ones in Serenity who ever made it rain!"

"I guess it can't do any harm." Eech let his leaf float away. "Okay. If you want to."

"Onion John," I said. He turned from looking at the

river. "Would three do it? Eech and I will help, if you want."

I waited while he thought it over. It would be terrible if after only a couple of hours I couldn't hear him right anymore. I remembered the trick was not to be so tight. I relaxed. John finally nodded and started off. I didn't have anything to worry about. I heard him. He made sense.

He described to us that even one person could manage, as far as that went. Except the fewer there were, the harder it was for each one. Those there were had to believe that much harder the procession would work. He asked us how we felt about it. Eech and I didn't see any harm in believing hard. When I promised we'd do everything we could, Onion John bounced right back.

"He wants us to fast all day tomorrow," I told Eech. "Not even breakfast. And to drink twice as much water as ever. And we have to meet him up here three hours before sundown."

"I can't get over you," said Eech. "The way you understand him."

It was wonderful, just to be able to sit around in a tree with Onion John and hear everything he had to say. He told us about his life. He was born in a high valley in some mountains there were way on the other side of Europe and everything they did in his home town was different, the way they danced and ate and spoke. John liked it there. Except that he wanted an acre of land where he could be by himself. And around his home, there wasn't any left.

An uncle of his was going to New York City and John went along, but there wasn't any land left there either. The way he came out to around Serenity was with the railroad, building the branch line that goes through the county. It was only a temporary job. He quit when he came to Long Meadows, about twenty miles below town, to grow vegetables in the muck fields, almost pure mud that they have down there. He enjoyed that, raising fine celery and onions. But it wasn't the same as having his own place.

So it was like coming home, for Onion John, when he found the two acres on Hessian Hill where nobody minded if he settled down. It was because of all the rocks, John figured, the place was empty. John used the rocks to build his house and before long the garden he grew had everyone startled. Especially the onions he turned out which was the way he got his name.

Along with the vegetables they bought, John found enough people around town who wanted him to keep up their lawns and shrubs at thirty-five cents an hour. He refused to take any more. He figured the price he set twenty-five years ago was about right and any extra they gave him would be charity. He thought everyone around Serenity was nice enough, letting him stay up on Hessian Hill all by himself, and he didn't want anything extra. It was impossible for Onion John to imagine a nicer place than Serenity, friendly as all the people were.

That's why he was so glad, and he shook his fist at the thunderheads, we were getting together to make it rain. It would help everyone in town.

"Anyway," said Eech, as we climbed down out of Onion John's sheepnose tree, "I don't see where it can do any harm."

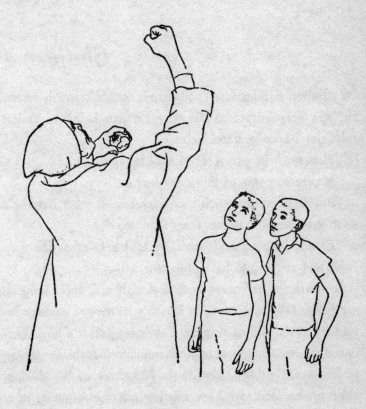

Chapter 4

My father, though, wasn't so sure it couldn't do any harm. He was very surprised the way I'd caught on to Onion John, how I understood him.

"That must be pretty exciting," he said.

"It sure is, some of the ideas he has."

"But making it rain that way, somehow or other it doesn't seem very sensible to me. Does it to you?"

"Except it just could work." I told my father the way John tied rocks into his apple tree.

It was in the hardware store that night and I was helping my father take inventory. In Rusch's Hardware we take inventory at the end of August. That's my father's idea compared to most stores where they count stock at the beginning of the year. Getting ready for the fall, there's a big change-over in the store anyway, moving out the summer merchandise, garden tools and fishing equipment and picnic stuff. What you start to feature is guns, axes and saws, animal traps and such. So in addition to rearranging for the new season, and finding out what's on hand, and what there is to reorder, we take inventory. When we take a rest from counting, my father and I talk things over, all sorts of things. It was one of those times I told him about Onion John, and how he shames his apples into growing.

"And you've got to admit, Onion John brings down some of the best early apples we get in town."

"He certainly does. But don't you think that might be a coincidence, Andy? Onion John's a great gardener. He'd grow good apples even without rocks."

"Maybe the same coincidence will work if we try for rain. As long as we get wet weather, what's the difference how it's done. You can't go anywhere without hearing about the dry spell, how serious it is."

"It's bad, there's no doubt about that. We stand to lose twelve to fifteen hundred dollars. In this store alone. If the farmers don't make it, we don't."

"Then what's the harm of trying?"

"There's no particular harm," my father smiled, "except for someone who might be going to the moon."

I laughed. Every time my father mentioned about going to the moon I saw myself in a space suit with my head in a bubble.

"What's the joke? Actually, there's any number of people who will be going to the moon, Andy, during your life time. Think of it. Why shouldn't one of them be you?"

"But a chance like that. You can't take it too serious."

"Why not? You're good in math. And if you keep going there's no reason why you can't make it up to M. I. T., the college we've talked about in Massachusetts."

"The Institute of Technology?"

"And once you're out of there," he nodded, "with a good scientific background, you can go anywhere. Even to the moon. There's no reason why you shouldn't take that seriously. As serious, anyway, as you do Onion John."

"Except Onion John's now. He's here in Serenity. And it's tomorrow afternoon, the procession. The moon's way ahead, it's years from now. Even if you want to think about it."

"You have to start sometime, Andy. Taking a sensible attitude toward what goes on. And the sooner you begin, getting your mind trained to see the logical reason for things, the better chance you'll have. That is, if you're at all interested in going to the moon."

"Who wouldn't be? Except it's so far away."

"Even if it is, I don't think cooking up a storm with Onion John is any way to train yourself. The harm is that you may get confused."

"I'll watch out," I promised my father. "And if I do, would you mind if we tried with Onion John? We've just gotten to be friends. And it would make him happy. And everyone else too, if his idea worked."

"Well, no, I don't think I mind." My father picked up

the clipboard that had the list of all the different items. "If it's nothing you really believe in. And you just go out there for the fun of it."

He started to check through his sheets to find out where we left off. I figured I had to tell him how it worked.

"You can't go out there for the fun of it. It's not like a ball game. John says you have to believe in it, hard."

"He did?" My father looked over the top of his clipboard. "Well even so, I guess this once won't be so bad. Besides, we'd better get back to work."

Mostly inventory gets done at night when there's no customers. It's all counting. If you try to take care of trade and at the same time keep a lot of numbers in your head, chances are it'll take twice as long.

As it is, we put in a week to ten nights to go through the place. There's over five thousand different items in our hardware store, not counting all the sizes in each item. Mostly it's me and my father working together, except for two nights when Walt, who clerks for us, stays on.

The nights we put in seem a good way, to me, for the summer to come to an end. The store's always dark, with only one light on because we don't want people to think we're open. And it's a little like we were in a big barn counting over our own kind of harvest, all the different things we have. Some of them are old, the wooden spigots for instance we keep for cider barrels and wine. And some are new, just out. like electric eye door openers. Going down the shelves, with all the shadows climbing around and the night dead quiet except for us counting, inventory is the most serious time we have together, my father and I.

He might say, "Lag bolts? Six inch?"

Then I answer, "Two dozen, plus one, two, three, four, five. Twenty-nine in all."

He says, "Check. Lag bolts, four inch?"

I'm up on the rolling ladder we have that goes down the length of wall behind the counter. I go over them and I look down. "Four and a half dozen of the four inch."

"Four and a half dozen." He writes it on his list that's held to his clipboard. "Right. Now about lead screw anchors?"

We go on for about a half hour that way, him asking and me giving him all the answers, between each break. But that night he stopped five minutes after we got started again.

"Talking about rain," he looked up to me on the ladder, "you know, don't you, there's a perfectly sound scientific way of making rain. Did you ever hear of seeding clouds?"

"Somewhere I did." Any idea that came from my father would certainly satisfy John. Long as it brought damp weather. "But I forget how it works?"

"What they do is, they scatter dry ice."

"Makes you think of snow, doesn't it?"

"So it does. But the purpose of seeding a cloud with dry ice is to chill it. Some of the tiny particles freeze and start

falling, picking up other droplets as they come. Until each one collects a full sized raindrop, like a snowball rolling down a hill. That's the process. And multiplied a couple of billion times for every cloud, you get rain. That's the way they do it."

"Sounds like a pretty clever way."

"It's certainly logical. And a lot of times it works."

"Not all the time? Why not?"

"No, not every time. There must be too many different

factors to hit. Wind, temperature, different seasons, dust in the air. There's a lot goes into getting it right."

"But tell me," I came down a couple of rungs on the ladder. "How do they know when they do get it right? I mean, suppose it does rain. How do they know the difference, whether it's because they seeded or it just rained anyway?"

"Well, I don't know if they can ever be absolutely sure."

"I see." It seemed to me like there could be as much coincidence to it as with Onion John, hanging rocks up for his apples.

"But at least, Andy, it's a reasonable approach. You can see the sense to it."

"I can see that, sure. No matter how much rain John would get, tossing the mayor around instead of dry ice, there'd be no sense to that. So why don't I explain it to John, how to do it your way? We could get dry ice from Eechee Ries, out of the soda fountain down at the drug store. Maybe enough for a pretty good shower."

"It's not that simple," my father shook his head. "The spraying's handled out of an airplane. A special crew, and special equipment, there's a whole outfit you have to call in to do the job."

"Of course, there'd have to be." I must've sounded pretty silly to my father, as if the three of us could ever toss dry ice high enough to hit any clouds. I climbed back up the ladder. "I guess we'll just call off the procession and leave it up to that outfit. Whenever it gets here." At least I could tell John something was being done. I found the place on the shelf where I was working. "I think we're up to pliers, aren't we?"

"Pliers," said my father. "But we're not hiring any such outfit, Andy." I turned to listen. "A job like seeding clouds costs thousands of dollars. Serenity can't afford to take that kind of a gamble. It's too big a deal for this town."

"But then, if not that, what are you going to do?"

"Nothing. We're going to let the weather take care of itself and get back into the hardware business. Back to inventory and pliers."

"Right." At least with pliers there wasn't anything you had to decide about them. My father asked me, "Long reach duck bill pliers?" I said, "Nine." And he said, "Check!" We went through regular slip joint pliers, ignition pliers, long chain nose pliers, cutting nippers and diagonals. As long as we stuck to the hardware business, my father and I, it was pretty easy knowing what to do. And working there together with the night getting late, we finished up the shelves behind the long front counter.

My father asked, "Knuckle joint planes?"

I said, "Three."

"Ries's," said my father. That's the way we knocked off every night, to go down to the drug store. My father'd have a cup of coffee and I'd have a plate of chocolate ice cream. We turned off the light and our steps sounded louder leaving the store, the way they always do in the dark. Outside, the full moon traveled through the big thunderheads that still hung up there in the sky.

"I've been thinking about tomorrow afternoon," I told my father. "I think we ought to go ahead with Onion John. As long as you don't mind."

"You still think so?"

"Well, there's a lot of sense to dry ice but there's nothing you can do about it. That's one thing. And even if we could, dry ice doesn't work any better than Onion John when you look at the coincidence. And with Onion John it's cheaper. There's not so much of a gamble. And it would certainly help the hardware store, if it did work somehow. And everyone."

"I wouldn't worry about that." My father looked up at the sky and he spoke quietly. "We probably will get rain. The seven o'clock news said we were going to get a break in the next thirty-six hours. A storm's moving in from the northeast."

The moon was gone for a second. It came back to turn the night white, and our faces like chalk, and the shadows along the street went sharp and black.

"Then I certainly think we ought to go ahead."

"In heaven's name, why, Andy?"

"Well if conditions are so favorable. I'd just as soon try when we got the odds on our side. That makes it better."

"Andy!" My father kicked a piece of rock off the pavement, into the road. He put his hands in his pockets and he walked away from me, down Water Street.

I caught up with him. "What's wrong?"

"Only me." He laughed down at the sidewalk going past. "I ought to be able to get this over to you. Why you can't go back to playing with the moon up there and the clouds, as if you had them on the living room carpet. Seems easy enough until I try."

Usually this is the best part of inventory. When we go down to Ries's after working on a job together. I didn't want anything to come up between us.

"You got it over clear enough. If you don't want me to go ahead with Onion John, I won't."

"That's not the point, Andy. Of course you can go ahead. If you're not persuaded, then I'm certainly not going to forbid you spending the afternoon with Onion John. It's not that important."

"Unless we get rain."

"Well, we can wait and see how that works out."

Mrs. Ries was behind the counter. I asked her to please be sure not to serve Eechee any breakfast. She couldn't see the reason why Eechee should miss all his nourishment. And rather than go into any more explanations, I told her never mind. It was simpler to take care of it myself.

Chapter 5

I was down to High Street by seven o'clock the next morning. And I got hold of Eech before he swallowed anything except, he told me, a little toothpaste. That couldn't hurt. I held on to him all day long, hardly passing up a faucet without taking a drink. We were hungry and waterlogged, getting up to Hessian Hill.

The procession couldn't start until sundown, and in the three hours we had there was plenty to do. First thing when I met Onion John, was to say, "Hello." He said hello, and I asked him, "How are you?" He had no complaints except for a small crick in the back, and I asked him, "What's new otherwise?" There was nothing new otherwise. And I was certainly glad to hear it all. Testing him out, everything he said still made sense.

Most of our time went into finding the right kind of torches to carry. These had to be young cedar trees just four years old. They had to be cedar because the wood smokes a lot and the smell has a lot of carry to it. And the reason for four years old was the last wet summer we had, when the river flooded, was four years back. So it stood to reason, any tree started that year would be best for getting more wet weather.

Walking across fields with Onion John and into woods was as good as going for a hike through a mail order catalog. Almost everything he came across had some use to him. John pointed out rocks, trees, bushes and even a black snake that were good for all sorts of things, for lumbago and making soup and improving your eye sight. That's the reason the sack of his was always bulging. He was forever picking up samples.

We found the cedars we wanted in a swamp in back of Tracy's farm, right below Hessian Hill. From the rings they had and the smell, and even the taste after he chewed on a couple of leaves, John gave us his word they were the best four-year-old cedars he ever saw.

The next we had to do was meditate. This was to get us into the mood of believing hard and there's nothing to it. You sit down and keep still and you think over anything you did that was wrong or bad. It took me a little while to decide. Finally I thought about missing the fly ball in the Rockton game. How much wronger can you get? And then I thought about taking a peek at Bo Hemmendinger's arithmetic paper, the last test we had at school. Which was bad enough. I had both points covered and I was ready to quit.

Except John and Ries kept going. I thought Eech was

carrying it a little too far. He never did anything all that wrong or bad to take the time he did. Waiting for those two, I meditated a little extra. About my father. And about Technology. And going to the moon. I always had in mind to stay on in Serenity and run the hardware store the way my father did. And leaving was a new idea to get used to. That's as far as I went meditating, when Onion John came out of his trance. He sang us a hymn.

It was the hymn we had to use in the procession. We had to learn it. And we couldn't, neither Eech nor I. The voice John used, way down deep like he was singing in a barrel, we couldn't match that. And the words were impossible. I couldn't get through the first three without fetching up lockjawed.

"Can't he do the singing?" Eech gave up. "And us come in for the drums. Boom. Boom. We could do that."

"We can't go," I gave him Onion John's opinion, "unless we sing. Otherwise he's going to have to hold a one man procession." Moving his hands like he was playing six games of checkers, John explained how one man held a procession. "It takes a lot of running around he says, but at least everyone in it is singing. That's important."

"Pete's sake." Eech scratched his head with both hands. "After all the fasting and the water we've drunk! Tell him we have to go along, Andy."

I thought of a song we knew that might do just as well as the hymn. We sang it for John, Eechee carrying the

46

melody and me doing the slides. John thought the tune was all right. And when we promised him there wasn't a wetter song in the English language, that fixed it. We arranged that he'd sing his special hymn and we'd sing my idea which was, "Anchors Aweigh, My Lads, Anchors Aweigh."

The problem was settled just in time. We heard the closing whistle of the new factory down the river, General Magneto. The afternoon was still and clear enough for the blast to carry all that way. We hurried to get started because the procession had to reach the creek just as the sun went out of sight.

John led us to the very top of Hessian Hill, on to a clean grazed over pasture, and we spread apart in a line with about fifty steps between us. We lighted up our torches and John was right, I never saw cedar burn so gummy black and strong. The idea of the smoke was to attract the attention of the thunderheads. Heavy and curling, the smoke had the look of young clouds starting out and that was something they'd notice. And the dry peppery smell the cedar sent up, that was to give the clouds some idea of how burnt it was down here, how brittle and dry.

The sun was headed straight down, when we lit our torches, burning a big ragged hole in the thunderheads. And the torches seemed to work. The whole valley turned roaring red. There wasn't a sound on the top of the hill, except some yakking crows, but the piled up flame spread out in the sky and the gold and the purple made you want to cover your ears. It looked as if the clouds were raging to see what we wanted.

There was a yell from John, "Advance!" and we took out. John's hymn started and he turned to wave his torch for us to get going. I heard Eech sound off with "Anchors Aweigh" and I joined in. I was extra light, with more float to every step, coming off Hessian Hill. That could come from not eating all day. Or it's what happens when you take to singing to a lot of clouds.

All the way down to the creek, we walked only along the crests of the hills so that we threw the longest possible shadows. Because that's what they eat, clouds are interested in shadows. Some we cast down the slopes below were better than a block long. And on top of them, the shadow of the lifting smoke off our torches built us up even bigger. It was a surprise how good a procession we were, just the three of us, once we took on all that size.

The sight of us almost wrecked a truck. We were going through a field on the Bemeth place, where the corn was still low on account of the drought, when a big two ton job came around a bend in the road below us. The driver must've went rigid. He jammed into a ditch and stayed there while we went singing out of sight. He had plenty to listen to. John's heavy voice went rolling over the country like there was a church leading us, with its windows open. I never heard an organ go any deeper.

Straight down it wouldn't be more than half a mile to

the creek. The way we went though, keeping to the crests, it was three times that distance. The lower we dropped, the more the slopes evened out and the less stretch we got to our shadows. But then we started to hit more hollows, where it was darker and the lights of our torches showed up better through the trees. That gave the procession as good a look as before.

We reached the bridge at Conroy's Bend right on time, just as the sun touched down on the Munkachunks. We tossed our torches into the Musconetty, to show the clouds that's all they had to do to put out the burning and the dried up smell. All it took was a little water. And then came the sacrifice, which was a way of saying please when you ask a favor.

At least years ago, hundreds, this part used to be a real sacrifice. Back then, they'd take the prettiest young girl around, a sort of Miss America who didn't know too much and hadn't dated around a lot yet, and they'd throw her into the water with a stone around her neck. The up-to-date modern way is to throw in the most important man in the procession without a stone so he has a chance to get out.

Onion John elected himself to be the sacrifice because he was a man, at least, without considering who was the most important. Eechee and I agreed. It would be a lot easier for Onion John to come home dripping than either of us.

We fixed up a launching platform with an old plank

we found and a branch we used for a pole. We balanced the two on the rail and John climbed aboard, crosswise, with his hands in his pockets for the smooth roll that'd give him. Eech and I started "Anchors Aweigh" and we lifted. John went barreling down the incline, picking up speed, and he was out beyond the rail hanging over the water, when he howled.

I almost dropped the pole, not knowing what happened. John tried to wriggle back. He got a finger hold on a beam of the bridge and he yelled for us to lean down on our end.

"Why?" yelled Eech.

"He wants to come up on the bridge again."

"He can't walk out on us now." Eech didn't move his plank. "This is the best part."

"He says it's all off," I told Eech. "The whole procession."

John was sorry and he apologized. He forgot his water stone. This was a clear piece of quartz you could almost see through. By rights it should be in his pocket when he got sacrificed. John left it back in his place and there was no time to get it because the sun was half gone. The whole procession was spoiled, he was afraid. It would never work. There was no reason to drop him in the water.

"There sure is," said Eech. "I want to see him splash. I've been waiting for this all day long."

"That's no good reason to dump him. The reason we got to dump him," I explained, "is the radio. After what the

51

forecast says, that ought to balance out the water stone."

"Did it say rain?"

"By tomorrow morning. And he'll feel terrible, when it comes down. If we dump him, now, he can take the credit."

"He sure can. You're right, that's a much better reason."

"Then let's," I said. "Let go."

The plank swung out of Eechee's hand and the pole out of mine. John roared as our launching platform flipped over the rail. The roar ended in a gurgle and in the splash that came up, Eech and I got almost as wet as Onion John. The point of his knitted hat came out of the water and went straight up until John stood with the creek to his middle, staring at us.

"Don't get mad," I asked him. "It really is going to rain."

John shook his head and let out a circle of spray. No it wasn't, he said, the procession was spoiled.

"But look, John!" I had to get him to finish the ceremony some way. "Long as you're in there, can't we see the end. So we'll know what to do the next time."

Next time, John told me, he was going to handle the procession all by himself.

"Then we'll never get a chance to see it all. Can't you show us now?"

With the drip coming off his nose and chin, John shrugged his shoulders as if to say, why not?

This is the way he finished off the procession. He stood

in the creek and he sang his hymn very slow. He took off his outside overcoat and filled it with water. He carried it like a bag over his shoulder and he came back up on the bridge. Eech and I took corners of the coat and we helped him toss the water out to make a big wet splotch across the dusty planks. Then he dropped the coat over the bridge and let it float downstream. The coat going down the river was supposed to be the body, the way it happened in the old days, of the sacrifice. Finally he said a short prayer and with tight fingers he touched his forehead, both shoulders and the exact center of his stomach.

"Amen," he said.

"You're not sore?" I asked him.

He didn't answer. But from the look on his face and the droop of his mustache, he wasn't happy. I hated to think we mightn't be friends anymore. But I was sure he'd see I was right to dump him, next morning when it rained.

He lifted the point of his hat. "Well, good day," he said, each word perfect.

"See you tomorrow," I said.

We watched him start up the hill through the dark that was gathering along the creek bottom. He dripped as he went and sloshed. He swung his sleeves at the bushes along the road, giving them the benefit of how wet he was. He stopped to take off his hat and he wrung it over a small flower.

That was as much water as came out of our procession.

Chapter 6

The next morning turned out dry.

"Eighty-two in the shade," my mother looked around from the sink when I came into the kitchen. "You boys must've slipped up someplace. The sun's a furnace."

"But how can that happen?"

"We used to believe in ants," she said. "Stepping on them. It never worked."

"That's not what I'm talking about!"

"Great day!" My father came through the door. "Where's the umbrellas, Andy? I thought we'd need them this morning."

"So did I."

"Too bad." My father shook his head at all the beautiful sunshine in the backyard. "This is going to be a shock to Onion John."

"You don't know the half of it," I told him. "He's liable not to want to talk to me anymore. The way today turned out."

54

"Just because it didn't rain?" My father sat down at the table. "Well Andy, anyone who thinks he can turn on a cloud the way you do a faucet, he ought to expect a little disappointment."

"But he didn't think so. That's just it. He forgot his water stone. John was positive it wasn't going to rain. It was the radio. That's what I was counting on. The radio was wrong."

"Was it?" asked my mother.

"Now that I think of it!" My father put down his orange juice. "It was."

"How can that happen?"

"Well, they're only human on the radio." My mother sat down with us.

"Don't they have barometers?"

My father finished his orange juice. "Yes, they have barometers, and hydrographs and isotherms, a lot of those things."

"How come none of them seem to work as well as John's water stone?"

"It's the way you look at it," said my father. "There's a big difference between Onion John and the radio. John thinks he can make it rain. The radio doesn't pretend any such thing. It only predicts when it's going to rain."

"Except it doesn't."

"That's right. They have their instruments and yet, sometimes, they do make a mistake. And they allow for it, for a reasonable margin of error. But with all his water stones and torches," said my father, "Onion John will never get it to rain. It's not an error. It's impossible. The point is, he can't." My father shoved his glass away. "Now finish your orange juice."

In the twelve years I've known my father up until then, and for three days later as well, he was always right. Three days later it rained. It started about five o'clock in the morning, before daybreak, the second day of school. The whole sky turned over like a tipped bucket and down it came in a steady wash until you couldn't see any raindrops through the window or any drip from the trees. Just water, streaming. The house shook with the roar.

Eechee Ries stopped by to pick me up for school. And my father came our way. We went downtown together in our slickers and raincaps and stopped at the bridge on High Street to look at the Niagara foaming over the spillway. The force of the water was frightening, the way it came at you over the falls.

"Look!" said Eech. Out of the foam twisted a cedar tree. It was small and burnt exactly like the torches we carried in the procession. Standing in the rain we watched the burnt stick of cedar go under the bridge.

"Onion John." Eech reached for me and I almost dropped the books I was carrying under my slicker. "He was going to hold a one man procession. Maybe he did It was John, he started this."

I looked at my father, who only smiled. "After all," I told Eech, "it's only a burnt piece of cedar. It could've come from anywhere."

Then, there wasn't any doubt about it. Over the dam it floated, getting lost in the foam and coming clear again to go under the bridge. It was Onion John's coat, the second overcoat he had. Eechee and I stared at each other. We wiped the driving rain off our face. We heard a far off hymn.

It was Onion John coming down Water Street. He didn't have any overcoat on, just an old piece of tarp wrapped around him and dragging on the sidewalk behind. He kept time with one hand, singing away happy as a bull frog.

"Onion John!" yelled Eech. "You did it."

Onion John lost hold of his tarp, waving back at us. He hurried up to where we were and Eech grabbed his hand. "Congratulations!" said Eech.

They shook hands and Onion John turned to me. He had this big smile on his face and I could see he wasn't sore about getting ducked. I didn't know whether to congratulate him for making it rain, my father was so sure he couldn't.

My father was wrong. And he knew it. He showed us he was wrong. He took John's hand and he held his arm. "Congratulations." My father didn't need any more proof. "This is just what we've been waiting for!" He patted the wet tarp on John's shoulder. "You did great."

No one could have appreciated Onion John more than my father. I heard him tell Mr. McSwain that the storm was better for Serenity than money in the bank. It was a shot in the arm, all up and down the valley, for the corn that was so stunted. It brought on a third cutting of hay. It came just in time. And there was just enough, without any floods or washed out roads. Even at the hardware store, my father guessed we'd catch up on the fifteen hundred dollars we were going to lose.

And the total cost of the whole thing was no more than John's two overcoats.

That wasn't any problem, even though right after the storm no funerals came along. John got most of the things he wore out of funerals. He attended them all because he didn't have any family of his own and he liked to take whatever happened, to anybody in Serenity, personally. He was the one who cried the loudest in a cemetery, to make up for not being able to say how he felt. And usually the family gave Onion John any men's clothes that were left over. But that was never the reason he came. John would come to anyone's funeral, no matter what size he was.

When no one died right then, I took care of the overcoats. Through the kids at school. They all knew it was Onion John started the storm, after Ries finished talking. Onion John was the greatest thing ever happened to Serenity, to listen to Ries. And the next greatest, because I understood him, was me. I began to get as much a reputation as George Connors, the star athlete we have, or Bill Berry who's double jointed or Bo Hemmendinger who gets the biggest allowance. So all I had to mention was that my friend Onion John needed overcoats. And they brought half a dozen down to the hardware store, the kids in our class, extra ones they found at home.

John picked an army officer's coat to wear on the outside and a long one with velvet lapels for underneath. They looked awful. But when John saw himself in a strip of sheet aluminum back there in the storeroom, he twirled on his heel. He called himself, a fine prince.

My father came through while he was at it, to pick up

three gallons of white paint. I couldn't understand my father. "Suits you perfect!" he said to Onion John.

"You don't really mean that?" I followed my father back into the store. "He looks all out of shape."

"I know." My father piled the cans on the counter. "But why spoil it for him? He's pleased."

"The way he looks, though!"

"You've got to humor him. He's a lot younger than you are, in many ways, or Dick Ries. And if he gets a kick out of those overcoats, well, it's the same as the pride he took when he thought he made it rain. He really believed it."

"Didn't you?" I watched my father as he went over to the desk to check on the order he was filling. I'd gone along as if my father and I thought the same way, now, about Onion John.

"Didn't I what?" he looked up.

"Is that what you were doing down at the bridge? You were only humoring him?"

"Of course." He straightened up. "Now, Andy! You're not going to tell me that you believed Onion John was the cause of that storm, are you?"

I did not answer my father's question. I said, "Well, it is hard to believe." Which was true enough. But I saw then that the best way to handle any question about Onion John, with my father, was not to talk about it. And it worked out all right, handling it that way, for a while.

Chapter 7

In Serenity, there's a lot goes on for Halloween. Some of it the kids think up for themselves, like almost wrecking things but never so bad that later they can't be fixed. Scribbling an automobile with a wax candle is part of that, and hauling off someone's gate to another part of town, and draping up a tree with a couple of rolls of toilet paper. Then there's prizes the Chamber of Commerce thinks up, for being artistic. You draw pictures with crayon on store windows, barns and witches and cats, and the best one gets five dollars.

The idea of the Chamber of Commerce is to keep everybody so busy coloring windows they won't have the time for any wrecking. But by working hard, the kids around Serenity manage to do both.

In addition to those things, there's four of us who give ourselves a party. We've done it for three years, Ries, Hemmendinger, Bitsy Schwarz and me. Soon as school starts we begin saving two and a half dollars each to chip into the party. It's a good deal for everyone but Hemmendinger, with his allowance. Eech gets it by working down at the drug store, and me with my father, and Bits by running deliveries for the A&P. It's not that we're hogs and we need all that money for food. There's a lot you have to spend for decorations.

That's because where we hold the party is in Hemmendinger's barn, or Schwarz's woodshed, or this year the plan was for our cellar. These are all places we know. And to make them look different takes more money than you'd expect in crepe paper and serpentines, and cardboard pumpkins, ghosts and skeletons. A lot of work goes into it too. We need about a week, getting together after school, to fix a place so it's hard to recognize.

The day before Halloween, the four of us do our shopping for the banquet. It's always the same every year. The main course is Mocha Cake which we have made to order down at Struhlmeyer's. It has to be a pretty big cake to hold all the writing on it, *Good Wishes, Rusch, Schwarz, Hemmendinger, Ries.* Then there's eclairs which are chocolate and vanilla cream puffs. For other courses we have Napoleons and two kinds of ice cream and rice pudding. The rice pudding's mostly for Bo, so we have that first the way you'd start off with soup. On the side, we have two little paper cups at each place, one filled with salted nuts and the other with chocolate creams. To drink we have Kiowa Club Ginger Ale which stings your throat if it goes down fast and makes your nose itch. It gives you the feeling it could be hard liquor you were drinking and that's an excuse for acting drunk if you feel like it.

It's pretty wild once we get going. All of us try to hold off long as we can, admiring the decorations and how nice the table is set. But that never takes too much time, seeing that everyone there worked at getting things ready. And soon as we start eating, that's about all there's left to do. The kind of meal it is, it slides down pretty fast. And we never can eat as much as we thought we could, which is always a surprise year after year. Once we're full, the party's about over except for drinking Kiowa Club and getting drunk and taking swipes at each other and yelling while we pull down the serpentines and crepe paper and the rest of the decorations we put up. The whole affair never lasts more than fifteen or twenty minutes.

It wouldn't be worth it, except for all the talk goes on beforehand during the weeks we save up the money. And afterwards, when we get out to spend the night around town and we tell the others what a swell party we had. Before and after, the party sounds like such a good idea that's why we decide every year to go ahead with it.

This particular Halloween though wasn't going to be the same exactly as the years before. One thing different, I had a date with my father for after the banquet and so did the other three. The Rotarys were putting on a program, which was a father-and-son evening where a magician was going to saw the executive secretary, Mr. Kinnoy, in half.

"I wouldn't want to miss a thing like that," I told my father. "Even if we have to call off the banquet."

"You don't have to. The program doesn't get going until eight-thirty. If you fellows start at seven, the way you plan, you ought to be finished long before then. You can have your party and come over to the club, both."

Along with that difference, the date I had with my father, was the invitation we gave to Onion John. It was Bo's idea.

"He's an expert, isn't he," Bo asked Eech and me, "on spooks and spirits? So if on the Fourth of July you have the mayor to make a speech, and on Armistice Day you have the American Legion and on Christmas you have Santa Claus, how about us having Onion John for Halloween?"

It was great with me, seeing Onion John was my best friend. And it was okay with the others, too, for John to be a guest even though that meant he didn't have to chip in or help decorate. There was always more than enough.

From the moment he walked into the cellar, Onion John changed the whole way we went at our party. Like with the decorations, this was the first time anyone besides ourselves had ever seen how nice we were fixed up. One step through the door, Onion John stopped and put down his burlap bag. He moaned as if he had a cramp. It was only because everything was so elegant. We followed him around

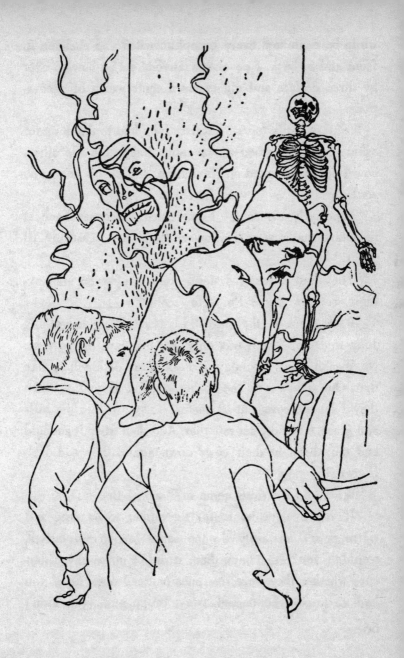

while he examined every pumpkin, witch and skeleton in front and in back. I never saw anyone get so bowled over by three dollars and eighty-seven cents worth of decorations.

We were ready to eat. But first John had to thank us for asking him. We stood at the table and I told the others how John appreciated our invitation with all his heart and soul.

"Especially his soul," I explained. "Because back at the start that's what Halloween was, the Feast of All Souls."

"They had a feast? I never knew they even ate anything, souls?" asked Bo. "How come?"

"Back there at the start," I passed along everything John told me, "there was only two big days in the year. No Washington's Birthday or Labor Day or anything like that. One day was in the spring, around May Day, when they'd let the cows out to pasture to go up into the hills and graze. They'd celebrate that. And then when it got cold and they brought their cows down again, they had Halloween."

"Where do the souls come in?" asked Bo.

"If you bring cows in for the winter to be snug and warm, you'd certainly do the same for your relatives, wouldn't you? And back then, it didn't make any difference whether they were live ones or dead ones. So if you had an uncle who passed away, or an aunt, you didn't leave them out in the wind and the dark where they'd get chilled to the bone. You invited them in to gather around the fire with the rest of the family. That's why, this particular night, they called it the Feast of All Souls."

"And what Bo asked," said Eech. "What do they eat, the souls at the feast?"

"John doesn't know."

Eech couldn't believe there was something John didn't know.

"I do," said Bits. "What they eat is filets."

Eech saw the joke before the rest of us. "Filet of sole." He roared and we joined in. I explained to John how filet of sole was a type of fish and he laughed too. But not for long. There was a danger, he had to warn us about, that came on Halloween.

"Can't we eat now?" asked Bo. "We can hear about that along with our rice pudding."

John held up his hands to keep us from sitting down. With all the traffic there was on Halloween, he told us, everyone holding open house for whatever souls they knew, there were others who tried to sneak in. These would be mean spirits who weren't friendly to anyone, such as hobgoblins, demons, witches and vampires as well as the ghosts of hung murderers. Halloween was the one big chance for such as these to come out of hiding and sidle in where they didn't belong, into the homes of decent people.

Eech figured that's how kids got started wrecking on

Halloween, when it could be blamed on these mean spirits.

"You're probably right." Bo reached for the rice pudding.

"Hold on!" I told Hemmendinger. "Before we eat, John says we ought to ward off any witches and the rest who are around. It's not only they can spoil the feast. They give you boils, distemper and dropsy."

"How long does it take to ward them off?" asked Bo.

It took about fifteen minutes. What we did was to fumigate the cellar. John pulled a load of laurel leaves out of his burlap bag and filled up an old ash barrel we had next to the furnace. Then he sprinkled this with a can of triple blessed oil.

"What's so triple blessed about it?" asked Bo. It was nothing but a rusty quart can of oil, the kind you'd get in a gas station. There were two wads of paper stuck into where the holes were punched. Bo pulled out one of the papers and stuck his finger in. We watched the oil drip back into the can. "Looks to me like plain crankcase oil, and plenty dirty too."

We gathered around while John explained. He whispered how he'd hidden the can of oil for almost a month underneath the pulpit of the Presbyterian Church. That made three Sunday's worth of psalms, prayers and sermons that flowed into it.

"You couldn't get much more blessing packed into one quart of oil," said Eech.

"I guess not." Bo brought a kitchen match out of his pocket. "Can I be the one to light the barrel?"

"With a match?" I stopped Bo because of what Onion John told me. "That's no way. You have to set it off with a piece of living fire."

The way you make living fire, John showed us, is with oak wood. Oak is worse than rat poison for demons. John brought two small slabs of it out of his bag. Also a thin round stick and a small bow, the kind you'd have for a bow and arrow. The thin stick gets looped into the bow and it gets held between the two slabs. And to bring out the living fire, you work the bow back and forth like you were playing a bull fiddle.

Onion John picked Bits and me for this job. Because Bitsy was the first born in his family, being the oldest, and I was the first born in mine, being the only one there was. John turned out the electric bulb we had in the cellar. In the pitch black, he said, "Advance!"

Bits and I held the stick between the two slabs of wood and pulled against each other on the bow. All we got for a while was a wheeze out of the stick as it twirled. Soon a glow began, in the dark, a tiny circle barely red. John started to recite, a bunch of jawbreakers like the words in that hymn he sang. John recited louder and louder as the circle got redder and louder still, when some of the wood shavings scattered around the bottom of the stick sparked up.

He dumped the living fire that sprouted into the leaves in the barrel. On account of the oil, most of what came out was smoke.

It was the smoke we wanted, John explained. Any fiends around were knocked senseless by the smoke. And to make it rougher on them when they dropped, John had us turn all the chairs upside down with their feet sticking in the air. I found a lot of other stuff to mangle them with. We bumped around in the dark and stuck up a rake, an axe, a bag of old golf clubs and a crow bar. For witches, the cellar was worse than a booby trap. By then it was pretty bad on us too, considering the smoke.

"Where's the door?" Bitsy started coughing. "Let me out of here!"

"For heaven's sakes!" It was my mother at the top of the stairs. "What goes on down there? Andy!"

The others headed for the basement door to the outside. I ran upstairs.

"Look at this kitchen," said my mother. It took me a little while, coming out of the dark, before I was able to look. Then I could see the big refrigerator and the stove all white and shining. And of course, a lot of smoke. And my father standing in the dining room door holding on to a magazine.

"Everything under control?" he asked.

"It's only a little fire in a barrel. It's almost out by now. We were fumigating for witches. With Onion John."

"John? Is he with you?"

It wasn't that I tried to keep it any secret from my father, the invitation. It never came up, any reason to mention it.

"I didn't know you ever had any older people," my mother said, "at your banquet."

"It's only Onion John's special," I explained, "when it comes to Halloween. There's a lot of history in what he knows. How Halloween started with souls eating. And why demons go flying around tonight. It's educational."

"And you're sure it's safe down there?" my mother flapped her apron at the smoke.

"For everyone but witches."

"Well look, Andy," my father folded his magazine. "Suppose you hop down there and empty the fire into the furnace. And we'll get going. It's late."

"But we can't. We haven't started to eat yet."

"Why not? It's practically eight o'clock. Don't you want to go to the Rotarys?"

"Sure. Who'd want to miss seeing the executive secretary get sawed in half? Of course I want to go."

"Of course he does!" My mother stopped waving her apron.

"All we got left to do, is eat. It won't take more than a couple of minutes."

"Besides there's the others," my mother told my father. "Herm Ries and Mr. Hemmendinger, they're waiting for their boys too."

"There's a half hour," my father looked at his watch. "That ought to give you enough time. Get going, Andy. I'll wait for you."

"And don't gulp," said my mother. "There's plenty of time to eat properly."

We had the cellar to air out, and the stuff to put away that we stuck up, and the fire to dump into the furnace before we started eating. And when we did sit down at the table, John took out of his second overcoat some big thick plumbers' candles, the kind sell at six for a quarter. Everyone had a lighted candle in front of his plate. As far as making the place hard to recognize the candles turned out better than the decorations. They changed even us. We looked more serious, each of us sitting in the dark behind a little flame.

At last, we started. Bo poured out the ginger ale. Then John stood up and held his glass and rattled away for a couple of minutes.

"He hopes we won't get distemper," I told the others. "And we get through the winter. It's a toast. Everyone has to give a toast."

Bitsy thought a bit and got up. "Melba," he said. "That's a toast." Eech got up and said, "French." I said, "Dry." And Bo said, "Buttered." We drank our ginger ale.

No one got drunk. We went to work on our rice pudding, talking about broomsticks, the kind witches ride.

I always wondered why a witch would ever pick anything so uncomfortable to travel on and John knew why. It wasn't a broom at all, back at the beginning. Only a sheaf of corn stalks, or wheat, or hay. This was the last bunch the farmers cut in the fields and they brought it home to save over the winter. It was called the Corn Mother. And the idea was to keep it through the time when the ground was hard with frost and couldn't grow anything until the spring came and the earth warmed up. Then the farmer would spread the Corn Mother out in the fields to remind the dirt how it grew crops the year before. It was a reminder. And if you didn't have the Corn Mother, if it got lost or stolen, there was a chance the dirt around a farm would forget what it was supposed to do and it would just sit there, flat as a super highway, not growing.

"So the witches would steal the Corn Mother," Bo finished up his rice pudding, "to cross up the farmers?"

John said that was the case. And the farmers would disguise the Corn Mother by putting a stick in it to make it look like a broom, as a way of crossing up the witches. They caught on though, as anyone can see by walking through a five and dime store and looking at all the stuff with witches on it. Everyone of them is riding a broom.

"Seems logical," said Ries. "If they were out to get something only to clean with, you'd see witches riding vacuums."

By then we'd worked our way past Napoleons, cream puffs and eclairs and reached our main course, the Mocha

Cake with the writing on it. John stopped to get his fiddle out of the burlap bag when Bo looked at the wrist watch he wears. "Holy Hannah. It's eight-thirty. My old man's waiting to go to the Rotarys."

"Mine too," said Eech.

"We'd better get out of here," said Bits.

"Without any cake?" Eech put down the eclair he was eating.

"Maybe we can get a couple of more minutes, if it's okay to be a little late." I stood up from the table. "I'll be right back."

The kitchen was dark when I got upstairs. My mother was in the living room having coffee with Eechee's Ma and Mrs. Hemmendinger and Mrs. Kinnoy.

"Your father's at the club," she told me before I had a chance to ask. "He went on ahead with Herman Ries and Mr. Hemmendinger. They're waiting for you there."

"If it's only a couple of more minutes, do you think they'd mind?"

"Pa asked me to give you a message. He says he's leaving this up to your judgment. You can come over whenever you're finished."

"Whenever?" That sounded like a good arrangement.

"Your father says you're welcome any time at all."

"Any time at all," I told the others when I got downstairs. They were relieved to hear there wasn't any rush. Especially when Onion John got started with his fiddle.

He was down at the end of the cellar where it was black except for a square red glow, like a stage, lighted up by the open furnace door. The violin John had was a wreck, patched all over with friction tape. But the sounds that came out were as good as new.

The number John played reminded you a little of "Old McDonald Had a Farm" except it was lowered a couple of notches and came out ten times slower. No one applauded when John finished and he looked at us again.

"What's it mean," Bitsy asked, "a song like that?"

Onion John told us the story of the song. It was about a man floating down a river in a boat who sees someone on shore that looks just like himself. It's as if he were seeing himself in a mirror. He tries to get into shore. But there's no way to manage the boat and it floats downstream. At the end, the one on shore waves and calls out. The man on the boat can't hear. And then he does. What the man on shore yells, in the last line of the song, is "Farewell."

"The story isn't much," said Bits. "But at least, you have to admit that the tune is beautiful."

Onion John had a couple of faster numbers, with more snap to them. There was a dance went with the last one. It was called a Clock Dance and John did it by going around in a circle, stomping heel and toe on the straightaways and scissoring his feet on the curves. He did it twice around, playing the fiddle all the while. None of us could even do it once without tripping.

By then we'd finished eating and the Mocha Cake that was left over spelled out a word. There was 'Hem' from Hemmendinger. 'Arz' from Schwarz. 'Ri' from Ries. And 'Ch' from Rusch. Hemarzrich. It sounded like Onion John's kind of word. But it didn't mean anything in his language either. We decided we'd make it a secret word. To mean— *trouble*. We arranged when anyone of us was in trouble, all he'd have to say was *Hemarzrich*. and the others would have to help.

In my judgment, it was time we got over to the Rotarys. The candles were burning out, anyway, and the brightest part of the cellar was in front where the moonlight came in through the windows.

It was when Onion John saw the moon that the big delay came. It was a perfect moon for making gold, full and near in a wide clean sky. But the miracle was, it came on Halloween! Never in Onion John's life had the two come together, on the same night, before. It meant, with his eyes wide John whispered, that our fortunes were made.

What decided us we had the time to make our fortunes was the sight of Mr. Kinnoy, the executive secretary, walking down the empty street.

"He's whole," said Bits. "They must've called off the program."

We went ahead with Onion John. He had everything he needed for stewing gold in his burlap bag, fern seeds and some sticks of lead, wood alcohol and some special stones,

76

the kind that philosophers used. By rights, we had to be in clean clothes but I found some sheets on the back line to wrap ourselves in. What with prayers and washing up and hymns and a little meditating, again, there was a lot of preparation before we had a pot filled with the proper ingredients.

John put it into the furnace. He poured wood alcohol in

the pot and a blue flame came out. He began a deep hum and he started to sway. Standing there in front of the furnace door, watching the flame, the four of us picked up his sway.

I heard a whisper. "Andy." It was my mother, far off. I listened and it came again, "Andy."

I swayed backwards a couple of steps and sneaked off without bothering the others. Before I got through the dark to the top of the kitchen stairs, my mother said, "It's after one."

When I came into sight she asked, "Is that my sheet?" She didn't wait for an answer. "This is no time to be playing ghosts!"

"We're not." I came into the kitchen and when I could see again, there was my father standing. "We're making gold."

My father interrupted my mother. "Okay, Andy. Ask him to leave."

"Who? Onion John? We wouldn't know how to go on without him."

"Get that man out of this house!"

"He's run into a miracle. It's the first time it ever happened in all his life."

"I don't care about that, Andy."

"Can't you humor him, just a bit more?"

"Not any more."

By now my eyes were accustomed to the kitchen and I

looked around at everything. The refrigerator broke out with a high hum.

"You just want me to get him out of here?"

"That's all."

"It's my fault we didn't get over to the Rotarys. We went by my judgment."

That didn't make any difference to my father and mother. They stood there looking at me in the sheet. I took it off and I folded it carefully.

"If you'd tell me what you want me to do," I asked my mother, "with the sheet?"

She took it out of my hands.

I went back down into the dark again. "*Hemarzrich*," I said to the others at the furnace. I never thought I'd get to use the word so soon.

It worked, for a secret word, the way we'd arranged. They put on the light. I told Onion John what he had to do. I figured he'd cry because he never cares who's around. Instead, he rubbed his mustache into shape.

They gave me their sheets, until I had an armful. Onion John picked up his burlap bag and the four of them left. I didn't know where to put the sheets down, not in a dirty cellar. I was lucky to find a laundry basket near the door. I took out the pot that was stewing in the furnace and I dumped it into the ash barrel. Everything, except for Onion John's stones. I picked those out so that I could give them back to Onion John next time I saw him, whenever that'd be.

Chapter 8

Next morning, my father was gone by the time I came down. I brought my lunch over to the hardware store, from school, and I found him with his two fingers pointed at a letter in the typewriter. It was pretty clear my father didn't want me to be friends with Onion John. But how bad, didn't he want me to be friends? Enough, so I shouldn't see Onion John any more? Or enough, I shouldn't even say hello to Onion John if I passed him on the street?

I started to ask but my father shook his head. "Not now, Andy. I'm in the mood to write the Biltgud Electric Company." That's an outfit sold us half a dozen popup toasters that poppedup slow. My father punched Biltgud across his typewriter, then the bell sounded and he swung around in his chair.

"It isn't Onion John worries me. It's us, the way we're behaving. You. We fix up a date and you just let it slide. And me. I go higher than a kite. That's not like us, is it?"

"No," I said. "Usually we get along pretty well."

"That's because any problems we have, somehow or other we settle them. That's what we ought to do here."

"How?"

"I don't know." My father looked at the typewriter and hammered with a finger at one key. "As a start, I'd say we ought to forget last night."

"I'm ready." It was little enough to get us settled, me and my father. "And I guess I ought to use better judgment."

"That's a good idea. If you're not so sure about it, suppose you talk it over with me. Beforehand. And not wait until one o'clock in the morning."

"All right," I promised. "And about Onion John?"

My father swung back to his typewriter. "I want to get this off to Biltgud."

So I didn't know where I stood with Onion John when I saw him heading straight for the hardware store late that afternoon. He came down Water Street right up to the front steps that led to the door. My father was busy with Walt, the clerk, setting up a display for shotgun ammunition. By taking a five-foot slide down the aisle, I managed to reach the door in time. I waved to Onion John and pointed, to get him to go back to the alley we have behind the store. Whatever my father had in mind, I was sure he wouldn't want Onion John in the store anymore than in the house.

I wandered past my father and Walt. Onion John was

going a blue streak by the time I reached him in the alley. For him, Halloween had turned out to be a disaster. It wasn't only the gold had him wrought up. When he got back to Hessian Hill the night before, he found his front door sitting on the roof. It was no more than what you had to expect on Halloween. And John wouldn't have minded, except both hinges were twisted off the door and one hinge was broke in half. He'd actually come to buy a pair of hinges, our biggest and strongest.

"Couldn't you find any out on the garbage dump?" I asked him.

John flopped his hands against his overcoat. He'd put in hours on the dump and the nearest he found to hinges, he said, was an old washing machine. I couldn't see where that even came close to what he needed.

"You wait right here," I told him. Luckily, the hinges were behind the front counter on the other side from where my father was with Walt. I meandered in and picked up a pair of six-inch, barn door strap hinges. I didn't hide the hinges, especially, except I held them against my side with my arm.

They were just what John had in mind.

"They'll last you a lifetime. Zinc plated steel. The best we have. Only eighty-four cents a pair."

John took another look at the hinges and judged they were worth twenty-seven cents. I said okay. I thought I'd chip in the rest out of my wages to make up, something anyway, for the fortune he'd lost the night before. John looked up from the hinges but the smile he had went over my head. "Well, good day," he pulled up the point of his hat as if he were leaving.

"Good day," came from behind me. My father stood with his arms crossed, holding on to his elbows, looking at us.

"John didn't come here for a friend," I showed him the hinges. "He's a customer."

"Then why didn't he come into the store?"

"I just didn't think that was any way to solve our problem, the way you feel about Onion John."

"But this way, Andy? This is no way! Hiding out in an alley."

Onion John had his purse unsnapped and was ladling out nickels and dimes. I acted business like, counting the change he put in my hand. "Twenty, twenty-five, twenty-six, twenty-seven." I gave my father the money. "That's on account. The rest is what I owe. On account of the gold we spoiled last night. I figured he ought to get a bargain."

I gave John the hinges. "I hope you find these satisfactory. If you don't, you can return them to Rusch's Hardware Store anytime at all and get a refund."

John thanked me, bobbing his head at my father, and he turned to hurry down the alley.

"Onion John!" my father yelled. John stopped and my father went after him. "Look here a second, will you. About last night, about the gold, about me stopping you. Don't get that wrong. It's not that I don't like you, John. It's only this whole business of making gold, well, I'm against it. It's wrong." My father looked around the alley to think how to explain it. "It could lead to inflation."

John turned to me to tell him what inflation was. I couldn't. My father showed us how if everybody started making gold, then it wouldn't be worth so much. And you'd have to pay more and more for the things you wanted.

"Those twenty-seven cent hinges," my father pointed at them in John's hand, "could go up to forty or fifty dollars with inflation."

John was amazed. He confessed to me he had never thought there was any danger in making gold. And for that matter, neither had I.

"He sees what you mean," I told my father. "Next when it comes time to make gold, he won't try to make so much."

"I'm glad we understand each other," said my father. "There's nothing personal to it, John. It's just a question of economics. Personally, I like you. I think you're a fine man."

John smiled because he was always proud to hear when anyone liked him. "He likes you too," I translated to my father. "He thinks you're a fine man."

My father nodded to thank John. The two of them had fine smiles.

"It certainly seems you two like each other," I said.

"Of course. Why shouldn't we?"

"Then why is it you can't get to be friends?"

"I guess you and I don't have too much in common, do we, John?" My father laughed. Until he looked at me. It turned into a surprised look, as if I'd just come into the alley. "Except one thing, of course. Andy. He seems to understand us both pretty well."

"If you were," I pointed out to my father, "friends that is, it would certainly help solve our problem."

My father nodded to me and then to John. "There's no reason why you shouldn't think of me as your friend, John. I wish you would. If there's anything I can do, I'd be glad to help. I'm not much at making it rain but if there's anything else, let me know."

John said there wasn't any help he needed. "But he's glad you want to be friends with him. And the next time you're up on Hessian Hill he asks you to drop by his place for a visit." I never imagined they'd get along this well. "Once he gets his door fixed, in a day or two."

"What's wrong with his door?"

I told my father the trouble John had for Halloween. "But these hinges, they're not meant for any house door." My father shook his head. "You'd use this kind of hardware on a barn, a whopping big barn door. Come on, John. I'll show you what you need." He started down the alley and then he slowed to turn around. "Or better yet. It's practically closing time. What say we let Walt close up? And us three, we take a run out to Hessian Hill right now. How about that, John? Let's go see what you really need up there."

I'd have called anyone crazy if they tried to tell me that morning I'd end up riding out to Hessian Hill with Onion John and my father in the same car. All the weeks I'd put in trying to keep the two of them apart, I could see that was wrong. What was more natural, if there's trouble between your best friend and your father, than to get them together?

John dusted off his best chair, a rocker with its runners off. But my father didn't sit down, he was so interested in seeing the inside of John's house. He stood in the middle of the room and he didn't move. Except for his head. This went around as far as it could go, then the rest of my father turned to see what was left.

John had built over an old foundation where somebody's house, long ago, burned down. He built of rock cemented together with clay and straw mixed. He kept it whitewashed outside so it looked nice.

Inside he had a complete wooden floor except for one corner where there was a hole. This was so he could throw cans down into the basement and anything else he couldn't burn that might turn out to be useful later.

"I think this is the first house I've ever seen," said my father, "without wall to wall flooring."

For furniture, John had a strong iron bed on which he

kept all his clothes. Sometimes, this piled up according to the number of funerals going on and made a good thick blanket to sleep under. He also had a beautiful table made of shiny mahogany with three legs and a barrel to hold up the fourth corner. There were four chairs, all whole. And a stove that didn't look very good but the way it burnt kept the place as warm as the Fourth of July.

But most of the room in his house, and there was only one room, was taken up by bathtubs. There were four white bathtubs side by side. John got them from the dump and it seemed a mystery to him why anyone would ever want to throw away a bathtub. First because they were beautiful and second because they were useful. For storing things. For bathing, John used a bucket. In one bathtub, John kept beets and cabbages. The other was mostly for onions and some potatoes. The third he filled with the dust he got from sweeping out churches.

"He actually brings dust in?" asked my father. "In here?"

I had to explain the dust wasn't for use inside. John spread it over his vegetable garden. The church dust was blessed, same as the oil he had, and it was as fine for his vegetables as any fertilizer.

The fourth bathtub was for newspapers. John used a lot of newspapers, not to read of course but to start fires with and to eat off. For these purposes, he collected the Serenity *Lamp* and the daily paper from down the river, *The Easton*

Globe. But for papering the walls, which he did every year, John used only *The New York Times.* Judge Brandstetter who subscribed to the *Times* told John it was the best newspaper. And John liked to use the best there was when he could get it. It made a nice quiet wallpaper without any murders, so far as you could read, or robberies.

There were only two decorations on the wall. One was John's patched up violin. And the other was a picture, painted red and gold on wood, so faded you had to come close to make out it was an old gentleman wearing a beard and a crown. This was *Saint Stepan.* He hailed from the same place as where John was born. The upkeep on *Stepan* was the biggest household expense John had. There was a candle lighted in front of him, night and day. And even though John burnt the candle in a glass and shoved a wick through the drippings, so they'd burn over again, the light bill on *Stepan* ran high.

"Who'd ever think there was any place like this in Serenity?" said my father. "But how about that door? I guess that's the only thing concerns us. Let's have a look at it."

John brought out his new hinges. And he waited while my father squatted to look over the door jamb.

"No sir. Those hinges won't do." My father stood up. "No hinges will do. This jamb here is split and it's rotted. There's nothing to screw on to. And even a new jamb," he examined the stone work around the door, "won't work. There's no studding here to fasten against. And if there

were, the wall's shot. The cement work, or the clay whatever it is, the whole wall's crumbling."

John said he had a lot of good red clay around, and straw, to fix it up.

"It's not worth it. Not with this kind of field stone. You'd have to start from the ground up, collecting stone." He turned to us shaking his head. "What you need, John, isn't just a pair of hinges. What you need is a whole new house."

Everyone needs a new house, John shrugged. "But as long as that's impossible," I told my father, "he wants you to explain what kind of hinges will work."

My father wasn't listening to me. He stepped backwards, to the outside of the house, and he looked the place over. "What Onion John needs," he said it all over again to himself, "is a new house."

"Yes," I repeated. "But as long as that's impossible—."

"It's not impossible." My father had a very quiet smile as he left me and Onion John. "Not at all impossible."

He walked slowly around the house. When he showed up at the corner again he stopped long enough to pick, with his forefinger, at the mortar between the stones. Then he came back to where we stood.

"Onion John," my father looked very happy. "I think you're about due for a complete change."

"How do you mean?"

"I think we ought to rebuild Onion John from the ground up."

Onion John and I stared at each other. My father talked like a magician.

"The first thing we're going to do is build Onion John a new house."

"Us three?"

My father laughed. "The Rotary Club. Ever since last summer we've been looking for a project. Since we put the raft off the beach down in the river. This is it! We'll build John a new house. The Rotary Club will."

"Would they ever do it?"

"There's a good chance they will. Onion John's been around an awful long time. Everybody likes him, the way he's taken care of himself all these years. And I think the time's come when the town ought to do something to help him. This is the project we've been looking for. I think they'll go for it. I really think every one of them will go for it."

John took me by the arm to ask if I wouldn't please explain.

"My father thinks you'd make a great project. For the people in the town. So you could have a new house up here."

Onion John said he didn't want anyone to go out of their way to fix his house.

"Not fix," said my father. "Brand new. You'll live like the rest of us. With heating and electricity, a refrigerator and running water and a new bathtub."

John raised his hands for my father to stop. A new house, he asked me, with another bathtub?

"And this one's going to be brand new," I told him. "Nothing off the dump."

John's eyes went wide. The new bathtub was what got him! My father and I stood there, in the growing dark, watching to see whether he'd laugh or cry. There's no telling, when he's happy, what he'll do. He started out with laughing. But then his eyes watered up and he cried too. He switched back and forth between one and the other and at the end his face was full of tears and teeth, both. He took my father by the shoulders and then threw a bear hug around him.

"He certainly thanks you."

"It's not me," my father laughed. "It's the club. They're going to have to vote on it first."

"But you're pretty sure, aren't you, they'll do it?"

"I'm almost positive!"

I couldn't hold back any longer. I knew the word now and I let it go. "Mayaglubpany!" John let go of my father and joined in. "Mayaglubpany!"

"What's that?"

"Friend."

My father tried the word a couple of times until he got it straight. And the three of us yelled together, like it was a high school cheer, "Mayaglubpany!" We finished out of breath. Then my father fixed up John's door, for the time being, and we left John standing out in front of his house, a shadow in the open door that was lighted by *Saint Stepan's* candle, waving at us.

"This might even be as much fun as making it rain," said my father. "What do you think, Andy?"

"I never imagined this." I watched the headlights stretching down the hill. "A thing like this! How'd you ever get the idea of building John a new house?"

"Well, for one thing, he needs it. That's sure." My father shifted into second to take care of the steep grade down Hessian Hill. "And another thing, Andy, to be honest about it, was you."

"Me?"

My father nodded. "If we're going to be friends with Onion John, there's only two ways to go about it. Either you go back with him into the fourteenth century some place. And you learn how to fight dragons."

"Who does any of that?"

"Or fumigate for witches, the same thing. On the other hand, we can bring John up, to where we live today. I just thought that would be more practical for John. And you too. And everyone concerned. It doesn't seem likely we'll ever run into a dragon."

"I guess not." I laughed. "And better than practical it's wonderful. The way it works out, you and John and the new house, all together. If it works out that way."

"It will," said my father. "I think it will."

Chapter 9

And my father was right. He passed along the suggestion about Onion John at the next lunch meeting there was of the Rotary Club. There's one every Friday. Before the Rotarys got through their main plate, which was creamed tuna on toast that Friday, a good many were talking about Onion John. Most of the talk was comparing Onion John with the raft they put out on the river. Most thought the house was just as good an idea, except it would cost a lot more.

Then they got around to how everybody would chip into the project from their different businesses, lumber and wiring and piping, and charge it off as an advertisement. That was one way to bring the cost down.

And another was the notion of everybody working on the house instead of hiring labor. For the whole club, all the members, to do the carpentering and the bricklaying and to build the place themselves. Not only would that help with the cost, it was early American. Back in history that was the way they had of putting up houses and barns. Every one pitched in for all of one day, back then, and they called it a building bee.

By the time the Rotarys got to dessert, which was slices of vanilla ice cream and strawberry sauce, there were a lot who thought this old-fashioned way was a good scheme even though the house itself would be up-to-date. At least it made the budget small enough so you could talk about it.

After lunch there's a business meeting where they smoke cigars. Before they got very far into it there was already a majority in favor of building Onion John a new house. And after my father and a couple of others got through reminding the rest how much John was liked around Serenity, and how well John took care of himself for so many years, everyone agreed it would be a fine project to build him a proper place to live.

Except for a while, Ernie Miller, the editor of the *Lamp*. Ernie thought that Onion John, so far as anyone could see, was pretty happy as he was. And besides Ernie wanted to know how would Onion John support a new house on thirty-five cents an hour to pay for electric bills and oil for heating and general upkeep. The new house would mean a different way of going at things, for Onion John, and Ernie didn't know how good that was.

There was a discussion to straighten Ernie out, and a resolution. All those Onion John worked for promised to pay him a dollar an hour, whether John wanted it or not, because no one can take any less except if he breaks the law.

After that, Ernie joined in and there was a unanimous vote to build John his new house. There were cheers when the meeting broke up. This was not for Onion John. Every week when there's a motion to adjourn the Rotarys cheer.

I knew all about the meeting even though, of course, I wasn't there. I heard a good deal from my father. And then I heard it all over again, with a lot more added, just by sitting back. Everyone knew I was Onion John's best friend. And the whole school wanted to talk to me about the things they'd heard at home. I listened to the same things again and again. I didn't want anyone to get the impression I was snooting him, just because I happened to be such a close friend of John's. Or because my father happened to be Andrew J. Rusch. So I let them go ahead.

"I heard your father was great," said Ries. "He said Onion John's a permanent part of Serenity. As much a part of the town as the bridge on High Street or the paving. We take care of one, your Pop said. Let's take care of the other."

"Is that what he said?" I'd ask.

Even Connors. Ordinarily with George Connors, if it's something you can't throw like a football, or you can't jump like an ashcan, or you can't race against, he acts like it's not very important.

"But when your father talked of the Umbangis," said

96

George, "how we send billions of dollars all over the world trying to civilize the Umbangis and natives like that! I thought it was pretty good when he said we ought to do the same for Onion John right here in our own backyard."

"Well!" I'd say.

But the real reason they were all excited was not so much what anyone said. It was how the idea opened up and spread. The Rotarys gave the project a name, Onion John Day. And as the news got around, a lot more than the Rotarys joined in. The ladies auxiliary and different women's clubs figured on putting up a canopy for breakfast and lunch and digging a barbecue pit for supper to keep the crowd fed. And then the High School band came in on Onion John Day to furnish music for everyone's morale while they were working. And then the ambulance corps in case of accidents, and then the other men's clubs, until practically everyone in Serenity was lending a hand.

It looked like Onion John Day was going to be as big as anything we'd had in town since the Seventh National Guard came back from Korea, when most of us were too young to get any fun out of it. The best part of way back then, so far as anyone recalled, was the free eats out in the courthouse square. On Onion John Day we were all piling in to do something, not just eat hot dogs. The seventh and eighth grades, for instance, it was us they were leaving Onion John's old house up to. We were going to tear it down. We were organized into the Demolition Committee

97

and a lot of comparing went on, between us, about the best ways of wrecking a house.

The whole of Serenity was organized. Ordinarily what you belonged to in town was your own family, or the class you were in, or the farm you ran or the store. During those weeks what you belonged to, if anyone asked, was a committee. Even the third grade, they belonged to the Debris Committee. That meant, during Onion John Day, they'd go around picking up nails and bits of lumber and strips of shingle that fell off the roof and they'd keep it all sorted out and in piles.

There was a committee for Trucking, for Tool Repair and Supply, and a Coffee Break Committee and Solicitation, which was where if something was needed, an extra tractor or chairs for the band to sit on, you went out and asked. Eechee was on Solicitation. There was a Press and Publicity Committee that Ed Maibee asked to get on because of the liking he had for envelopes, the taste of them. Press and Publicity sent out a lot of envelopes. There were always meetings to be announced and there were items had to be sent to the newspapers. There were even a couple of writeups came from Press and Publicity that were printed in the daily paper down in Easton, *The Globe*, how Serenity was getting together to put up a house in one day.

My father was on the Executive Committee. He was the Chairman. Onion John wasn't on any committee. It was a little lonely for him.

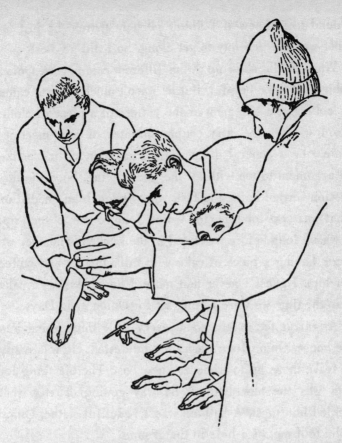

I saw a lot of Onion John, myself, on business. If the
Architectural Committee wanted him to look at a blueprint,
or Curtains and Slipcovers wanted him to look at yard
goods, naturally I had to go along. There was no other
decent way of talking to Onion John, except through me. It
took up a lot of my time. Not that I minded, handling a job
that important. The truth is, everyone at school and most

around town knew if I didn't pitch in there'd be just no other way for Serenity to get along. So I did my best.

When he did show up at the different committees, Onion John tried to be helpful. But he wasn't much when it came to looking at a blueprint or the pattern of a piece of cloth. Besides, after the first couple minutes of any meeting, there'd be a general discussion which sounded more like an argument to me with all the interrupting. Soon the discussion started going too fast, what Onion John needed or what was best for him, for Onion John or me to keep up. It wasn't long before we ended in the kitchen, wherever we were, having a piece of cake with milk for me and coffee for him. I guess I never had more different kinds of cake than the time we were getting set for Onion John Day.

As far as the details went, every little thing going into the house, Onion John wasn't too interested. He was ready to leave those up to whoever knew best. The big thing for him was the new bathtub he was getting. That's what tickled him most. A bathtub was a beautiful statue, Onion John told me, of a hole in the ground.

It almost ruined Onion John Day, the bathtub did, and even the friendship there was between Onion John and my father. We went up to Hessian Hill two days before the Sunday when the big day was going to be to check the plans for wiring the new stove. My father went to measure and I went along.

When we got up to John's place, there was an axe working in the woods behind his garden and that was John. We yelled and let him have the auto horn a couple of times and went into his house. It was warm inside, and dark and dry with a comfortable smell because of all the vegetables John had stored. With the day so wet, rain until mid-afternoon and now so overcast and cold, it was a good place to come into. We waited for John, in the shadows. The only light came from *Saint Stepan* and from a couple of cracks in the stove where the fire popped. We stood with our back to the stove, rubbing, to get rid of the chill we'd collected.

John came in with an armful of wood, laughing as if he'd just heard a good joke from somebody outside. But it was just because we were there. He dropped the wood and lit up a kerosene lamp and put a pot of water on to boil. He told us how nice it was we came to visit because he knew we were so busy with Onion John Day.

My father rolled out a set of blueprints and went down to his knees to go to work with a tape measure. I told John what was up, how my father had to check the electric wiring for the stove. John laughed as if this were even a bigger joke than the one he might've heard outside.

"Frolka?" That's what John called his wood stove. The name it had, lettered on the oven, was Frolic. John thought it was crazy putting wires into Frolic. All it needed was wood.

My father looked up at him with a smile. "You're not going to have to live with Frolic anymore. All that's over with, John. Schwarz is getting you a GL 124, the latest there is."

John was confused. He looked at me. I described how he could get rid of the old stove now that he was getting a brand new white shiny model, all electric.

"Frolka!" John hurried over and helped my father, practically lifting him to his feet. He set my father down in one chair and me in another. He hardly finished a word he spoke, fast as he went. It was hard to follow.

But one thing was clear. John wasn't going to get rid of any Frolic. He'd had the stove for eighteen years. It was more an old friend than just an appliance. It had a special way of cooking food, especially *pradzhnik*. And besides it heated the place. And besides he knew how to work it.

My father talked very patiently. How much cleaner a new stove was and how much easier, with no wood to chop. How the place would be heated with oil. About electricity, and how easy it was to work with nothing but a switch.

John shook his head, on and on, until my father said, "Think of Mr. Schwarz. It'll be a blow to him. He's proud of giving you that stove. How do you think he'll feel if you let everyone else in on this. And Mr. Schwarz, you take his stove and hand it back to him. He'll feel you have something against him."

He'll be sad? John asked me.

"Very sad," said my father.

John went over and looked at Frolic. He warmed his

hands over the top of it. Finally his shoulders lifted. All right, he turned back to us, he didn't want to make Mr. Schwarz sad. We could tell him he could bring his new stove and put it where the old one was.

"It can't go exactly there." My father rolled out the blueprints again. "Not without shifting the whole electrical circuit. The stove'll have to go closer to the wall." He pointed to how things were going to be. "That'll change the bathroom slightly. But even so, relocating the bathroom is a lot less trouble."

John wanted to know about the bathroom. My father explained how this was a small separate room with white plastic tile on the walls. John listened very carefully. Then he asked my father a favor, not to make any separate room for the new bathtub. The couple of times a month he'd be alone in the tub, it was a shame to hide it away in a little room by itself.

"He wants it out here." I hadn't realized, myself, what Onion John had in mind. "With the other four bathtubs."

"The other four what?"

"He thinks it'd be nice to have the five bathtubs right out here, all in a row."

"No, Andy. I don't think you or Onion John understands." My father worked the blueprints back into a tube. He slapped them against his hand. "Please tell Onion John that the whole idea is to build him a regular, respectable house. There can't be any four bathtubs in the living room.

103

Or five! Just one, tucked away in its own small room where maybe he'll enjoy using it more than once or twice a month." My father raised a finger. "Explain there's only going to be one bathtub in this house."

"The way his heart seems to be set on five," I said, "I don't think he's going to like it."

"Andy! Onion John, please take a look." My father spread the blueprints out on the table and pointed where there was going to be a sofa and a coffee table and an over-stuffed chair and a floor lamp. Together with a table for eating off and a kitchen arrangement at one end of the room, the place was pretty well taken up.

I had Onion John right, though. He didn't like it.

"He says he don't need a special table for drinking coffee, or those other things. He'd just as soon have the bath-tubs."

"John!" My father spoke word by word and loud. "It's not proper, or right, or civilized."

I listened to Onion John and got back to my father. "All he wants to know is, who'll it make unhappy. Anybody?"

"That's not the point. We're trying to get him to live normal and comfortable. Can't you get him to see that?"

I gave my father the last of what John said. "Long as it doesn't make anybody unhappy, he'd just as soon go and have the five of them out here in a row. And be happy himself."

"Great heavens." My father turned to look through the

window at the gray outside. "Who ever thought of this!"

John's back was turned to me, too. He warmed his hands at the stove.

I stood in the middle. It couldn't end here, my father and Onion John being friends. I sided with my father. After all, Onion John couldn't have a better friend, all my father was doing. And I sided with John. After all, long as no one else was sad why couldn't he be happy? There had to be some way to handle this.

"How about it?" I asked my father.

"Never mind." He watched the mist that was coming up outside. "Let me think."

"Onion John?"

He let out a word that turned six corners and doubled back on itself to end, the way it sounded, as if he spit. He didn't turn around.

I waited. I looked at what was in front of me. It was a story in *The New York Times* that started WAR CLOUDS GATHER IN INDONESIA. I looked to see what the war was about. A gobble came up outside, not so far away, like the call of a turkey.

"That!" I said. "You know what? I think that's an English bird."

Pheasant, John turned.

"Cock pheasant." My father looked at both of us. "Close by!"

We heard another gobble. Without a word, my father

dashed out the door. By the time John had his gun from behind the stove my father was back with the twelve gauge over-and-under shotgun he carries in the trunk of his car all season. In his other hand he had a pair of rubber-footed hunting boots.

No one said anything about the argument. My father changed into his boots. John rummaged underneath his bed. He came out with a long beautiful feather, green, red and white, the tail feather off a cock bird. He ran it into both barrels of my father's shotgun.

"What're you doing?" asked my father.

"Makes your gun shoot straighter, John says, the tail off a bird from the year before."

John opened the fire door of the stove and tossed the feather in.

"Isn't he going to use it on his own gun?"

John explained you could use only one feather for one gun. He didn't have any others. "Well, thank you," said my father, "for giving me the break, whatever good it is."

Outside it had turned sharper, the cold, and a real fog had climbed over Hessian Hill. John led us beyond the rise of the hill and we dropped toward the swamp below. We spread out. My father and Onion John kept pace with each other, about fifteen yards of brush between them. I went on a little ahead, with the idea if I kicked up anything they'd have plenty of time for a shot, bird-dogging it.

We worked our way very slowly down the side of the

hill, the three of us in a triangle. Every few steps we pulled up to listen for the cock again. The cover was very low and in the fog rolling past all you could see was my father and John and me. We were the only things black and solid. Besides us, there was only gray winding into white here and there and then fading out.

We started quietly into the swamp. No one spoke. There wasn't anything to talk about, here. The gobble sounded again, off to our left. My father waved for me to go in, the two of them holding their elbows out, loose. I changed direction, feeling out each step in the boggy ground. There was a whirring blast stopped me, startled, even though every second I'd been expecting a bird to break cover.

"Yours, John!" my father yelled. "Take it!"

The bird rose, past the sound of the shot that came from Onion John. It glided into the lighter gray above. There was another shot, my father. The bird pulled up as if it just remembered something it left behind, in the brush below. It came down scrambling, the way you start downstairs two steps at a time and then you go out of control.

"Gosh!" yelled my father. "Wasn't that beautiful?" he asked me as they came up. We were on our way to where the bird dropped. I was just about to answer when it came, another exploding whirr. The bird rose out of nowhere and headed straight for us.

"John!" yelled my father.

There was hardly time to swing a gun. John was wide.

And low, with the bird practically overhead. My father cracked me with his elbow as he turned. He shot. I didn't mind the quick hurt in my cheek. I watched the bird. It started to fight for a hold up above, reaching with its wings for fog to hang on to, and missing. The pheasant fought its way down and disappeared.

"Andy!" My father was on his knees in front of me. "Did I hurt you?"

"No. It's okay."

He watched for a couple of seconds waiting to see if I was going to let go. I never felt less like crying. Not with the three of us, after how it was up at the house, having such a good time.

On his knees still, my father looked up into the sky. "That was it!" he said. "That was absolutely it. I never thought I'd ever get a shot like that."

John kept saying, again and again, like a prayer, a long slow word full of s's.

The two of them went on repeating themselves. We collected the birds and started back for John's. "I practically took that shot off my hip. Right off here." He showed us. "I didn't think it could be done. You don't suppose—" Whatever his thought was, it ended in a laugh. "You don't suppose," he started over again, to John, "your tail feather had anything to do with it."

John was absolutely positive. It was exactly how the tail feather was supposed to work.

108

"Well," said my father, "I don't know."

When we got back to the house, with the two pheasants turned bright as rainbows under the light at the table, my father said it again. "I don't know. It sounds weird to me but if that's what you think, we'll leave it up to you."

It turned out he was talking about the bathtubs. "We won't close in your new bathroom, John. We'll put it over in the corner, behind a screen. Whenever you want to have it out in the living room, you can take the screen away."

That sounded fine to John. And the other four bathtubs?

"Well, we're going to redo the cellar downstairs. It's almost going to be another room. Suppose we put the other four bathtubs down in the basement where you can go and admire them, whenever you feel like it."

John thought for a second and then he agreed. It sounded like a fair arrangement. He and my father each took a pheasant and they shook hands. John came with us to the car and he watched us take off.

After a while, my father stopped thinking. "No," he hit the steering wheel, "there's just no sense to it!" I didn't know whether he was talking about the tail off the pheasant or the bathtubs. But by then, it didn't make too much difference. We weren't broken up, the three of us, and Onion John Day was still coming up, only two days away.

Chapter 10

You gotta get up.

You gotta get up.

You gotta get up, this morning."

It was still dark at five-thirty of Onion John Day when the massed bugles blew from the courthouse tower. This was the opening event, Reveille. Anyone who could play a trumpet or a bugle, from the High School Band or the Veterans', collected at the courthouse to wake the town up.

I lay in bed and listened, to the end. There wasn't one wrong note. It sounded real professional, the opening event.

Except halfway through pulling my pajama top over my head, they started up again. I hadn't seen on the program where there were going to be any encores. I figured this one was a blast for the extra heavy sleepers.

But when they blew again for the third time, there didn't seem any sense to it. It came just as I got the cap off the toothpaste. By then, for sure, everybody in town was on their feet.

That was the end of Reveille. But a single trumpet, sweet and slow, came through when I was brushing my hair. It was "Home On The Range." It was Ben Wolf, from the sound of it, the number he always played at band concerts.

What happened was thirteen horn players showed up. No more than four could crowd into the tower. They played in shifts. Three times four is twelve and the one left over was Ben Wolf. So they let him play any solo he wanted. It was useless to keep grinding out Reveille over and over.

I had to make the first car out. It left High and Water Street, according to the time table in the printed program, at 5:52 AM.

Everything on the time table was for odd minutes like that, 1:03 or 10:28. It was Mr. Donahue, his notion. The good of it was no one'd keep track of the odd minutes, he thought. And they'd get where they were supposed to be ahead of time. At 1:00 instead of 1:03. Or at 10:25 instead of 10:28. That way the schedule wouldn't get all fouled up with people straggling around. Besides it sounded better organized, like we were running a railroad.

I left the house at 5:43. The dark was slacking off now. The sun was scheduled to rise in just an hour, at 6:44. A lot of the houses along the street had lights on. Past the bright windows, through the quiet, I half ran the four blocks downtown. You could feel the hurry there was, in the still morning, everybody tearing toast and gulping coffee and wading into cornflakes.

111

John's place was a lighted square, from the road, his window. When we opened the door the only thing on was the candle for *Saint Stepan*. He was in front of the candle, kneeling with his head down. We waited at the door and watched the shape of Onion John as he said his prayers. He crossed himself. He came to his feet and he blew out the candle. It was the first time I ever saw Onion John's house black, with no flame where *Stepan* was.

A match struck and the lamp over the table lit up the house. And the man who stood there turning down the wick so it wouldn't smoke, he was a surprise.

Onion John was wearing only one overcoat, the underneath one with the velvet lapels. And instead of heavy sneakers he had on a pair of patent leather shoes, a little pointed, that used to belong to Grandpa McSwain who died at the age of eighty-four. And the hat he put on, now his prayers were over, was a fedora practically brand new. The fedora was creased exactly right, the way you'd expect.

But when he talked, Onion John sounded the same as always. He told us how good we all looked. He got out chairs for us to sit down and visit.

"Visit?" Mr. Kinnoy looked at his watch. "It's 6:03. We're the Committee on Personal Arrangements, John, and we're two minutes late as it is."

Late, John wanted to know, for what?

"For the schedule," said Mr. Kinnoy.

John apologized he kept us waiting. He took longer than

usual with *Saint Stepan* for all the things he had to be thankful about. John used another minute, explaining, before Mr. Kinnoy interrupted.

"We're due out of here at 6:22." The Committee on Personal Arrangements, he explained, had to empty the place of all John's things. "But your valuables, John, I wish you'd take care of them yourself. You can stow them in my station wagon."

John nodded. He looked around and picked up an old iron skillet off the table and tried to make up his mind whether it was valuable.

"Please!" said Mr. Kinnoy. "Just what's important."

John nodded. From the wall, he took his old fiddle. And his shotgun from behind the stove. From under the bed he came up with an old shiny spade that had its fifth handle, he once told me, fitted into it. He put this stuff on the table and on top, the picture of *Saint Stepan*. Then a prayer book. It was the only book he had. But today he had another one, the printed program of Onion John Day. It was the size of a small magazine with a green cover that had a drawing, without too much resemblance to it, of Onion John. Inside, there was mostly advertisements. But John couldn't read anyway, neither the program nor the prayer book. So the inside wasn't very important. That finished the pile of what was valuable. I helped John carry it all out to Mr. Kinnoy's wagon. In the little light spreading outside he asked me what a schedule was.

"Look," I pointed.

There was a far off rumble. And over the hill came a glare that spread through the sky until suddenly it narrowed down to a long beam of headlights. Right after, came another pair of headlights shooting high in the air. They leveled off as the top of the hill was reached. They were the first trucks from Burke's Lumber Yard, a couple of big two-ton trailers. Behind them came a smaller panel truck, from Struhlmeyer's bakery. Then a sedan, smaller still. This would be Mrs. Ries and a car full of ladies, including my Ma. They and the bakery truck were in Food and Refreshments, breakfast division. In the still morning, all you could hear was the roar of the convoy.

"That's a schedule," I told John. "They're right on time. It's the most important thing happens today. Everyone keeping up to schedule."

Now we had a moment to visit, I started to ask him why he was wearing such a new kind of outfit. John left me. He hurried into the house. Before I even reached the door, he was out again with the rocker in his arms, the one without any runners. He went out of sight around a corner.

Inside, Personal Arrangements was in full swing, taking the bed apart, emptying the bathtubs, moving out the table. I gave a hand with the table, tipped over on its side so it could be jockeyed through the door, when John came back. He put his shoulder to the corner George Connors was holding, and shoved.

"That does it!" said George. "We're wedged."

Mr. Kinnoy looked around from the bed where he was working. Mostly to get John out of the way, I imagine, he said, "How about those things on the stove, John. Will you handle them?"

John was done with the stove by the time we got the table unstuck. He swept the pots off the top into a burlap bag and pulled pans out of the oven until the clatter filled the house. Because we blocked the door, he threw the bag out the window. He was back with us at the table just as we were starting to move. He leaned into it and we were wedged tighter than before.

"You know what I think?" Mr. Kinnoy held on to the headboard of the bed and glanced out the window. "With all those cars starting to come in, John, you ought to go out there and show them where to park."

There was a good deal of traffic, from the noise. John agreed. He had to crawl underneath the table to get out of the house. And we had the place just about empty, the chairs and a cupboard, his clothes and the bathtubs, we had the stovepipe down and we were just starting to move Frolic when we heard a crash. It was someone's fender, sure, got collapsed.

In a second, John stood at the door again. Mr. Hemmendinger who was in charge of Parking and Traffic thought it best if he came back to check if the house was cleaned out right. John wanted to help with the stove. But

Mr. Kinnoy shook his head to show that we had it under control. John looked around the room, bare now with only some sticks of firewood left in the corner. He watched us carry Frolic out the door.

"6:29," said my father. You could hear him a quarter of a mile around. He'd come up in the loud-speaker truck of Berry's Television and Radio Repair. That was going to be my father's job all day, keeping the schedule going over the loud-speaker. "The house is clear for salvage," he said. Anything useful, like doors and windows, had to be collected by Salvage, before the house was torn down. "And breakfast! Chow's up for anyone hasn't eaten."

John wanted me to go with him to find my father. It was getting light now. There were a couple of dozen cars parked. And just coming in off the road were three school buses. One would have the Band. And another, my crowd, Demolition. I couldn't remember from the program who was in the third. My father was easy to spot, in the one truck that had a horn on top. Ben Wolf was with him. Besides playing a trumpet, Ben Wolf's a bookkeeper who works down in the new factory, General Magneto. He was helping my father to keep the bills straight and the receipts, as well as the schedule. The two of them had a lot of papers in the truck.

"John!" My father saw us. "Well, that looks better."

John straightened the brim of his fedora so it stood out flat all around.

116

"It's yours!" Now I knew why it was familiar. "It's your best hat," I said to my father. "Next to the one you bought last Easter."

"John and I thought he might dress a little special today, considering how special a day it is. More like everyone else."

John nodded to show how much he agreed with that idea. He asked me to put a question to my father.

"Because he's not on any committee, he wants you to tell him what to do. He's ready to try anything."

"The first thing's breakfast." My father pointed over to where they'd set up a tent with wide awnings for the ladies to cook under. "You hungry, John?"

John nodded as if the most important thing to be, according to the schedule, was starved. It was my mother who waited on us, at a counter made out of planks laid over sawhorses. We'd eaten, my father and I. He had a cup of coffee and I had a glass of milk. But John had the whole works laid out for him, juice and Crusted Toasties and doughnuts and a platter of coffee cake. "Or for the guest of honor," my mother stood with her hands on the counter, "we could manage eggs. With ham or bacon?"

"John's only breakfast I ever saw," I told my mother, "is salted fish or sardines and black bread and a powerful piece of cheese. And onions of course. He always has an onion."

"I don't know about the rest," my mother looked into the cartons behind her, "but we can certainly fix him up with these." They were as big as baseballs, the onions she put on the counter, and they were beauties.

"Not for breakfast!" My father pointed with his spoon. "Not onions."

John glanced around at the three of us. He told me that my mother didn't have to go to any extra trouble. He shoved the onions away, slowly because they were such good lookers. Then he said he didn't want any onions. And he started with the orange juice and Crusted Toasties.

I left my milk and I went around Onion John, to sit on the other side of my father. "Why don't we tell him he can go ahead and eat the onions?"

"But he doesn't want them."

"That's only what he said."

"Why would he do that?"

"I think he's trying to act like everyone else. The way we want him to. Just to please us."

"But maybe he doesn't actually want any onions."

"He's a friend of mine, Pop. The thing is, I know about him."

"He's a friend of mine, too." And of course, that was so It was the best thing could happen. "And do you know what I think," my father took a swallow of coffee. "I think he's changing."

"All of a sudden, overnight."

"It's a start. Those onions, he may be losing his taste for those. Once he starts living differently, you never can tell. He might end up a completely different kind of human being, Onion John."

"Actually?"

"I think he might."

At 6:44 there was a growl that rolled up as the band started its first number, right on schedule. "The World Is Waiting For The Sunrise." The timing couldn't be any more perfect because the sun rose too, on schedule. The bright yellow rim of it climbed the road to Hessian Hill.

Onion John put down his spoon to listen to the band. It looked to be out of politeness. My mother told him the music was only for morale. And Onion John went back to his Toasties.

I watched the light of the gasoline lamps under the canopy thin out. With Onion John Day only starting, there were already a lot of changes in Onion John. If he kept on trying so hard, it could be that he might change into a completely different human being. My father's guess was as good as mine. Or maybe better, now that he was a friend of Onion John's. That problem at least was solved. The way the two of them got along, and how fine they understood each other.

Listening to the music and watching the sun come up on Onion John Day, both at once, I figured the way they got along was enough to be happy about.

119

Chapter 11

Tearing down John's house turned out to be as good as anyone ever expected. It started with fifteen of us, all from my class, battering away from the inside.

The battering ram we had was a long four-by-eight-inch beam they were going to use for the ridge pole of the roof. Our job was to get the walls of the house to fall outward, out on the ground where the rock could be cleaned up easy. No bulldozer could get inside the house to do the job. The seventh and eighth grades could demolish a house fast as any bulldozer, if it came to that, once we got going.

We all hung on to the long piece of timber and waited for the next one to make the first move.

John started it. He was with Mr. Ries and Donahue and a couple of others who were standing by inside to see we were careful. John looked up from Mr. Ries' wrist watch. "Advance!" He picked up a sledge hammer. "Advance!" He took a swing and put a crack into *The New*

York Times. John let loose with another thud and daylight showed.

"One and a two," said Eech. "Three!"

The line of us let heave. And the timber rammed through, clean past the stones of the wall to push out a small jagged triangle. We tried again, and a whole chunk of wall came splintering down. From then on, no one held back.

Except it's by mistake, how many chances do you get to wreck anything? And when you do put out a window with a football, or get shoved through a picket fence, the next thing you have to do is run. Up at Onion John's we had a chance to concentrate, to work out different ideas how to demolish. When we finished with the battering ram, everyone had their own special approach to wrecking.

George Connors used an old baseball bat that only lasted a couple of swings and split. Some tried with a sledge hammer but Eech and I figured those were too heavy. And some with an axe or a regular hammer, which we thought were too light. Eechee and I used a crowbar. He supplied most of the muscle, behind me, at the end of the bar. And me up front, I did the guiding. We had power and accuracy both.

We didn't try so much for speed, like the others walloping away. We found the way to score was to pick out the right rock to hit. So we studied our way along and twice with a single swing, we started landslides that left gaps in the wall a yard wide. But the touchdown we made, the real home run for us, was the wall behind where the stove used to be, the west wall. The key rock had the shape of a horse's head and all the other rocks branched away from it.

"Wait!" Eech waved everybody to the other end of the room. "Hold them back, Mr. Donahue," said Eech. "You ready, Andy?"

The place was quiet and all I said was "Check!" We took the sideways step we'd developed and got our backs into the swing of the bar as we let it out.

Crunch. There was the dry grinding sound of a crack that started slow. Then another crack opened and built into a roar. Everything was hid. The inside of the house went yellow and white with the dust rolling back. The roar kept up. It got louder. Until I could see it was the people outside, through where the wall used to be, cheering.

The entire wall was gone. The roof would've come down if it weren't propped with beams. Eechee and I walked out through the rubble and shook hands with anyone who wanted, including Onion John.

He said we did fine.

"It's the way you built it." We couldn't take all the credit. "I never saw a house any better built for tearing down."

"8:11," said my father through the loud-speaker. "Cleaning and Grading. Get a dozer over to the building site. Demolition's complete. Move that rock out of there."

122

"8:24. Ditching. The water line's marked to the spring. Start your back hoe at the house."

Every time my father made an announcement there was a lot of rushing around. From the cars where they were parked in the corn field next to John's, or from the job that was finished to the one that was getting started. And with the band going every twelve minutes, "The Washington Post March," or "Poet and Peasant," or "Oh, What A Beautiful Morning," or "The Thunderer," Onion John Day got to be as busy and happy as a fair. Everybody was dressed in their roughest clothes, loud shirts and heavy boots and aprons and overalls, until you hardly recognized them. A locomotive engineer dressed in stripes and a high peaked hat turned out to be Judge Brandstetter, of all people. You had to look close at who came along.

Mostly when I saw Onion John he had somebody stopped to ask what time it was. I was sorry I told him about the schedule. He was forever on the go. Everywhere my father sent him, the different chairmen thought the most important place for Onion John was somewhere else. And John was anxious to get there. The truth is Onion John was a waste of time on a job, and material. It took time to explain to him what to do. And when he got started, he broke things. Even the two-inch galvanized water main couldn't stand up to Onion John. It split like a hickory nut soon as John put a Stilson wrench to it.

It would've been better for everybody if he didn't try

so hard, to change. First, he wasn't very good at it. And second, I didn't see anything wrong with the way he was.

At 9:17, my father said, "Plumbing. Make all your water and sewer connections into the cellar. We're waiting on you."

At 9:42, my father said, "Ditching. You'll find the cesspool marked out for you at the northeast corner."

At 9:53, my father said, "Masonry and Cement. Start your mixer. The foundation will be ready for you in exactly seven minutes."

And at 10:07, Onion John said, "Stop!"

It was clear enough for everybody to understand. Then the loud-speaker went garbled with shouting and yelling, until my father hollered for me to come over.

There was a crowd around the loud-speaker truck. John explained to me, he came there looking for my father because we were all in danger. My father wasn't around the truck and John took a chance at talking into the microphone himself.

"What danger?" asked my father. "What's wrong?"

All I started to get from Onion John was how beautiful the day turned out. That was true. The sun was way up, straight above the hills where the Musconetty comes from. And without clouds, the sky looked clean as a stretch of washed blue slate that was waiting to be written on. It was a little warm for November. But that didn't take away from how beautiful the day was.

"But what's the danger," asked my father, "in a pretty day?"

"Because the sun's shining," soon as I understood I told my father, "John says everyone has to work on the west wall in the morning, and on the east wall in the afternoon. To keep their shadows from falling into the foundation." I listened some more and it sounded a lot like Onion John, before he started changing. "If they let their shadows fall in, John says, they could get crippled, or sick. Or killed."

My father relaxed. Over the loud-speaker he said, "The alert's over. This is the all clear. Everybody carry on." By then I had the rest of the story from Onion John.

Years ago, he told me, anyone building a house or a castle, if they wanted it durable, would cement a live person up into the walls. Then they found that closing over a spot where someone's shadow fell was as good as having an actual man or woman built-in. As far as durability went. And it was just as hard on the person who's shadow it was. He'd be doomed and get feverish, sooner or later, or have a bad accident and die or get killed. John didn't want anything like that to happen, not to anyone who was kind enough to come up and help him.

"John, you can stop worrying," my father put his arm around John's shoulder. "Nothing like that can happen here. We're protected."

John waited to hear how.

126

"We're covered." John followed my father's arm sweeping across the top of Hessian Hill. "Completely protected by insurance. Comprehensive Liability and Workmen's Compensation."

Protected even against shadows in the cellar, John wanted to know.

"It's the fullest protection there is," said my father. "Against anything!"

John tried the word. "Compranshy," was as far as he got. The words had a powerful sound to them, he thought, like a very strong charm. He was glad to stop worrying, with everyone protected by Comprehensive Liability and Workmen's Compensation.

"And from now on," said my father, "why don't you stick around and help me." He gave John a clipboard to carry, full of lists and plans. "That way I can explain things as we go along and we won't run into any more trouble."

I watched them go off together. Over at the house they spoke to the man who was working the chute at the back end of the cement truck. My father and Onion John walked around the foundation watching how the stuff poured. They ended up at the east end, with the sun at their backs. They were tall men, the two of them, and their shadows stretched far across the wet cement on the cellar floor.

I went back to Carpentry where I was a junior helper.

At 11:02, the cement work in the cellar was done.

And ten minutes later, at 11:12, the frame of the four walls went up. It had taken a couple of hours to assemble these on the ground, two-by-fours nailed together and braced. But setting the frames up took only a few seconds. There was a cheer went up with them because all of a sudden the skeleton of a house appeared and for the first time it looked as if Onion John's new home was taking shape.

At 11:52, Onion John got a new name. This was at a conference Press and Publicity had, over at the loud-speaker truck, and I was asked to show up.

I'd never been to a press conference before. All there is to it is people standing around and talking. My father was there with Onion John, and so was Ernie Miller and Mayor Weltershot and a couple of others who were on Press and Publicity, including Ed Maibee. He was standing by, I guess, in case someone had an envelope to lick. There were editors from the weekly papers in the towns around. And one reporter, from the daily paper in Easton, *The Globe*, who took notes from what my father was telling him.

This was mostly about the number of people on the job. Close to two hundred and fifty, my father said, including women and musicians. The reporter, whose name was Mr. Jonah Davis, thought there had to be twice that from the look of the crowd. The extras though were only spectators, people who drove over special to watch. Or cars passing by that stopped to see what was going on. There was an ice cream man, to take care of spectators, and another fellow selling balloons.

"Did you ever expect this kind of circus," the reporter asked my father, "when you started out to build Mr. Claiblin his house?"

"Mr. Claiblin?"

My father looked around to where I'd been standing since I showed up. "Here's Andy now." The reporter nodded as if he were expecting me.

"Who's Mr. Claiblin? Not Onion John?"

"According to your father."

"We found out in New York," said my father. "Through the immigration office there."

"Mr. Claiblin?" I asked John.

John shrugged to say, No, and he nodded to say, Yes, both at the same time. He circled his fingers in the air to show that the name was close enough to be right. We shook hands, as if we were introduced.

"Pretty warm for November." I didn't know what else to say, getting introduced to someone I knew all my life.

John thought it was warm. And I kept studying him, how he looked in his new name, while Mr. Davis and I sat down on the running board of Mr. Berry's truck to have an interview.

"Just to get settled about you first." Mr. Davis looked at his notes. "You're in the seventh grade and you're going to major in mathematics. You're interested in science. And you're headed for the Massachusetts Institute of Technology."

"How'd you know?" I always thought an interview was where they asked you questions instead of telling you.

"Your father. That's correct isn't it? You're going into physics?"

"Years from now. But what's this got to do with me? What's happening here. I'm not what you're going to write about, are you?"

"You're part of it. I want to be able to tell who you are. I understand you know Mr. Claiblin about as well as anybody in town."

"Onion John?" I still couldn't connect him with a brand new name.

"Mr. Claiblin." He waggled his hand. "Onion John. It's the same thing."

"I guess it is." I watched Onion John under his fedora hat, standing with my father for a picture. "Except he is changing. There's no telling how he'll end up."

"Changing?" Mr. Davis crushed his paper inside out to find a clean side. "From what? How was he before?"

"Just fine," I told Mr. Davis. "There was no one else around who was like him. With his ideas. That's as far as I'm concerned."

"Well, you ought to know, you're his best friend."

"I guess I am," I said and that was the end of the interview. I couldn't see where anything I told Mr. Davis was worth writing up. But at least, I knew, I gave him the facts straight.

Onion John's name was what everybody talked about over lunch; fried chicken and cole slaw, baked lima beans, sweet potatoes and fresh cider, pumpkin pie and ice cream.

"What name does he use for his autograph?" asked Bitsy. There were a lot of spectators asking John to sign a copy of their program. "Onion John or Mr. Claiblin?"

"He signs an X," I said. "That could mean either one."

"And faster," said Eechee. "And easier, for him anyway, to keep up to schedule."

By early afternoon the schedule got to be a problem. Because of the crowds. The hills around and the fields were mobbed and more and more people kept coming. There was a big sign on Route 96 below Hessian Hill that read "Onion John Day" with an arrow, pointing. And up they came, those out for a drive on such a nice Sunday, with license plates from all over the state and from other states as well. Most of them, with their sticks of ice cream and balloons and hot dogs and picnic lunches, didn't think we could make it. They said we couldn't build the house in one day the way we planned.

On our own, it wouldn't make too much difference for some of us to come back on Monday to finish up. But with a big audience, what we had to do was make good. Onion John Day became like a championship. And to win, the committees broke apart and everyone worked at whatever job was going. A lot of times there weren't enough tools. And once even, the loud-speaker had to warn half of us to get off the roof where we were shingling on account of the house might cave in.

It gave my father and Ben Wolf a lot of extra work,

sorting things and moving help around where it was needed. And right behind them, everywhere they went, Onion John kept up with the clipboard he was carrying. Onion John or Mr. Claiblin, that is.

Whoever he was, it didn't change how he got along with my father. From up on the roof where I was shingling I saw them all over the place, the two of them together.

My father called me over, around 3:11 or so, and asked me if I wouldn't mind teaching Onion John a short speech in English, where he would accept the new house. It wasn't going to happen yet for four days. After the inside got fixed up with furniture and curtains, there was going to be a ceremony on Thanksgiving morning to give John the key.

"And it would be nice for him to say something everyone could understand." My father handed me a paper. "We wrote a couple of lines. I thought this would be a good time to go off with Onion John someplace, to help him memorize it."

I took the paper. "Where do you want to go?"

"Not me. I can't get away. You and John don't need me."

"Well sure, we could work it out together." The speech was only three lines. I showed it to John. He didn't think it would take him very long to learn. "We could get back in an hour."

"No, no, take your time. Get out of here and go off by yourself. Take the rest of the afternoon, you two!"

I could see my father was in the same fix as the other chairmen, as far as trying to work with Onion John around.

"The whole afternoon?" I asked him.

"Please, Andy. This whole deal's liable to fall to pieces if we can't keep it organized. Until we call you. Keep going until we've got this job licked."

John and I went off to find a quiet place to study. And there wasn't any, not until we got way in back of John's garden where we found the sheepnose tree was empty. We climbed up into that.

Dressed the way he was and with a new name, it was a little strange being back in the sheepnose tree with John. I asked him how he felt. He said he'd never worked so hard in his life.

"Just going around carrying a little clipboard?"

It wasn't the carrying, he said, it was trying to understand so many new things wore him out.

"Do you have to try so hard?"

Yes, John said, he had to do his best, with everyone else getting exhausted.

"Well, at least," I opened the paper, "this shouldn't be so bad." I read the speech off to him. "I feel happy and very proud that the people of Serenity have fixed me up in this fine new house. This is a good day to give thanks. But it is hard for me to say how much I appreciate all that you've done." That's all there was.

We sat in the tree and John learned the words, syllable

by syllable. The only problem was to keep John from putting in his own syllables, like *ovitch* or *owsky*. John tried hard. It didn't take long before the words started to come out clean with only a few extra grunts here and there and a couple of odd *z*'s. Tidying those up, in little more than an hour he was saying the whole speech so anyone could understand him.

From all the yelling that came over the loud-speaker, though, it sounded as if my father was still pretty busy. So I started all over to teach John the expressions he ought to use for his speech. "I feel happy," I taught him, "that's with your chin up and your arms stretched out wide."

"And very proud, is with a big smile."

To give him a start, I made out as if I were the speaker. "It gives me great pleasure to present these keys to Onion John—or," I asked him, "which is it, Onion John or Mr. Claiblin?"

There was an apple next to John, brown and shriveled from getting caught with frost. John picked the apple and turned it over in his hands, thinking, then he threw it away. The best thing he said was to ask my father. John thought Mr. Rusch would know best.

"But your own name! A thing like that, it's up to you."

He shook his head, none of them were his right name, not Onion, or John, or Claiblin either. His right name, when he pronounced it, was two blocks long. So it didn't make any difference what name was used, he shrugged, as long as it fitted the occasion. And who would know that better than his best friend, John asked me, Mr. Rusch.

John repeated about his best friend, Mr. Rusch. So there wasn't any mistake in the way I heard it. This was the biggest change that came along on Onion John Day. How my father was John's best friend. And this was one change I had to do something about. I had to get hold of the reporter from Easton, who's name was Jonah Davis.

I got the promise from John that he'd stay in the tree, to rehearse by himself. I climbed down and I searched all over Hessian Hill, where they were working at the house and all through the crowds that stood and watched. Mr. Jonah Davis wasn't anywhere. And no one I asked had seen him.

It looked as if he collected enough for his paper and he was gone. I thought to call him, but there wasn't any phone around. The best I could do was wait, until that night when I got to a phone. I only hoped that wouldn't be too late. I went back out to the tree where John was speaking his speech in a good loud voice and I went to teaching him the rest of his expressions.

By then, every time my father made an announcement there were cheers. There was a roar at 4:42 when the prime coat of white paint was done.

And another roar at 5:07 when the little roof over the front doorstep went up.

There was a roar at 5:32 when the last brick went into

the chimney. I don't know what the roar was about that came at 5:36. I didn't catch what my father said and what happened was inside the house. At 5:42 there was a rush for people to get into their cars. All the automobiles were shifted to make a wide circle around the house and they put on their headlights. From the tree the place looked fine, all lit up in the night that was coming, solid and white with a red chimney on top and a dormer window that was just for show because there wasn't any second floor.

In a little while the electricity came on inside the house, without any announcement, and there was another cheer.

In the dark, I couldn't see any of the expressions John was using or gestures. And I'd just as soon have heard from my father that we could come down. I listened to the words, so the time wouldn't be wasted, and to the wind that blew. After a while John's speech didn't sound so clear anymore because his teeth went to chattering with the cold. I figured if I couldn't see him, or hear him neither, he and I didn't have any other particular reason to sit around in a tree together. We started to climb down.

And my father said, "6:32. Right on schedule. Where's John? We're ready for John! Bring him in!" The house was finished.

The band played, "Mountain Majesty." They went through it once by the time we reached the house and had to start all over again. Walking through the two lines of people, I stayed with John. Everyone applauded. We

137

stopped at Mr. Kinnoy's wagon to get John's valuables. And then we stepped into the house.

There was nothing to see. Except people. All of Serenity was jampacked inside, Mayor Weltershot and Judge Brandstetter and Mr. Weems from the bank, and Kinnoy, Donahue, Ries, Ben Wolf, my father, so many people there was no house to look at except the ceiling. The ceiling was painted blue.

Onion John looked up at the ceiling while everyone applauded. Then they held off and waited to hear what he'd say.

No words came out of him. I knew what to expect, no matter how much he was trying to change. And that's what happened. He stood there and cried. The house kept still and everyone watched him cry, until Onion John reached out and took my father's hand. Then the applause came back. Soon the clapping was drowned out by cheers. And the storm really broke when those outside joined in. The auto horns picked up, hundreds of them, and it sounded like the top of Hessian Hill was blowing off.

Everyone who could reach John shook his hand. He kept up crying. With his arms going and the tears rolling, he looked like he might get himself pumped dry. He was still crying though, when the room went white with the explosion of a flash bulb. It was Mr. Jonah Davis from *The Globe*. I reached through the crowd for him.

"Hold it." He pushed me aside and studied through the

wire square he had on top of his camera. "Out of the way, please. One more!" He shot off another blinding glare and he bent down in the noise so he could hear me. "What's up?"

"The interview we had. One of the facts I gave you is wrong."

"Which one?" he asked me.

"Where I told you I was Onion John's best friend. The fact is, I'm not."

"No?"

"Not anymore."

"Thanks," said Mr. Davis. He promised to print the story the way it should be, how it was my father instead. That was the last I had to do about Onion John Day. I caught a ride on a car that was going back to town, with some people who weren't going to stay for the barbecue supper either.

Chapter 12

My regular hours at the hardware store are Wednesday and Friday afternoons, and Friday nights when Rusch's stays open along with everyone else in town. But I came down to the store from school that Monday after Onion John Day, special. Christmas was coming. And Rusch's was always the first to be set for the holidays. Our decorations are up by Thanksgiving and that causes a lot of comment from people.

So I thought I'd help to get started on the decorations. All that Bits and Eech and George Connors and the rest at school could talk about was what happened on Onion John Day, how good it was. And long before the three o'clock bell everyone had told everyone else, as far as I could see, all they could remember that went on. With the exception, maybe, of me. I didn't tell all that went on, not everything. It wasn't that I was trying to protect any reputation about being John's best friend. There was just no sense to it,

141

hashing over and over again the same things. I'd just as soon get busy with what was coming, like Christmas, and lay off after awhile what already happened.

Besides, there's a lot to dressing up a hardware store that's like getting set for a party. It's exciting. I don't get a chance at the windows, they're for my father to do or the different salesmen who put up their own displays. But inside where we have columns, we wrap those in red brick paper so they look like chimneys. I help with those. Then there's a fifteen-foot string of letters that spells MERRY XMAS I hang over the front counter, with two big red paper bells at each end. It's tricky, getting them up, but that's one of the things you learn in the hardware business.

I was on the ladder getting started when there was a thud at the front door. We'd been waiting for the afternoon *Globe* and when it hit, my father brought the paper in. He cussed Arnie Burke out, same as he does every day. Arnie rides route for the Easton *Globe* and he's phenomenal the tight weave he works into a newspaper. After my father got the knot untied and had a look at the front page, he whistled.

"Holy Hannah!"

"What's it got there?"

My father didn't answer. Reading the first page he walked back to where his desk was. I slid down the ladder and took off after him. But I couldn't see where it said anything about Onion John on the front page. All it had was, MOON ATTEMPT ASSURED BY NEXT SUMMER.

"What's so Holy Hannah?" I asked him. "Where does it have about Serenity?"

I helped him turn the page and there it was, right inside, three pictures and a big wide story. One picture showed Onion John getting pumped dry, near the end. One picture was from the morning, with John and my father and the mayor and the others. I was in the third picture. This was a full view of the house showing all the cars parked. I was one of those on the roof because you could see where the shingling was half done, and I was up there at the time.

Elbow to elbow, my father and I read the story and I was through first. I skipped till I saw the name Rusch. "A prime organizer of the event," the write-up said, "was Andrew J. Rusch, prominent merchant and Rotarian, who is John's closest friend in town." Mr. Davis had it the way I told him.

Then it said where the Onion John situation was brought to the attention of the town by me, "Andy Rusch, Jr." which was right enough. I was the one who brought it to the attention of my father how he and John might come to be friends, and that was the start.

"Nothing wrong there," I said.

"Wrong?" My father kept reading. "I'd say this was pretty good." He finished reading the write-up out loud. " 'For the next few days the house will be in the hands of various committees, mostly ladies, applying the finishing

143

touches to the interior. On Thanksgiving, Mr. John Claiblin will formally take up residence in a home that will only seem to be built out of sticks and stones. In reality, its basic material is the warm hearted good will and the generosity of the town of Serenity.' "

"Certainly is a nice end to the story." I got up from leaning on the desk.

"But this one," my father turned back to the first page where it had about the moon. "I never thought this story would ever start so soon. As early as next summer."

I left my father reading about the moon and picked up a full box of thumbtacks. I climbed the ladder again and went back to hanging Merry Xmas.

"Twenty-four thousand miles an hour," he said that's how fast the rocket'd go. "Think of that." When I put my mind to it all I could think of was—whoosh. "And in two years, Andy, after they land their first rocket, they expect to send a human being up there. A man!" He looked from the paper up to where I was on the top of the ladder. "Man alive, it's coming a lot faster than anyone ever expected. If you want to be in on it, Andy, you'd better grow up fast."

It was a joke the way he said it, so I patted the ceiling right over my head. "I don't have too much room left, not here."

My father laughed at the way I picked him up. "You're right. Not around here." He came over to the glass counter at the foot of the ladder. "You know, next summer. I've been thinking about next summer."

"About going to the moon?"

"About General Magneto. I was talking to Ben Wolf yesterday. He works there."

"I know."

"Ben Wolf was telling me, down there at General Magneto, that to run errands and in the stock room they make a place for boys that are interested. They let three or four have summer jobs, Ben was saying."

The thumbtack bent, the one I was using for the letter X. I tried with another thumbtack. "Is this okay?" I asked him. "The space between Merry and X?"

My father said the space looked good. "Ben drives it alone," he went on, "down to General Magneto everyday. He has plenty of room in his car. In case anyone took a summer job, there'd be no trouble getting back and forth."

I had the X hung up. For the next letter, M, I had to get down and move the ladder. But I stayed where I was.

"I thought it might be a good idea for you, to take a job next summer down at General Magneto."

"Me?" I was careful, turning around to face my father below, and I kept my balance. "Why would I want to go down to General Magneto? What for?"

"Considering the plans you have, Andy, where you're headed, it's certainly something to think about. To see what goes on inside a big industrial plant like that. You'd start

getting into the atmosphere, that way, of what you're going to do. It might be a good way to spend the summer, don't you think?"

"But summers, where I work is here," I told my father. "With you, in the hardware store."

My father stepped back from the counter so he could look at me better. He leaned against a table full of kitchenware. "I know, Andy. But this isn't where your future is going to be. A one-horse business like this."

"One horse." I sat down on the top step of the ladder. That didn't seem like anyway to talk about the thousands of different items below. Every one of them was useful. "What's wrong with Rusch's Hardware Store?"

"It's not this store." My father looked around. "The whole business is old fashioned. Every customer comes into a hardware store, you've got to find out what his problem is and figure out what to do about it. You've got to talk to each one personally."

"Why not? Most of them are friends of ours."

"Yes, but it's the super market, that's the big way to operate today, where the customer takes care of himself. What's new, modern, the thing that's up to date is self service. And it's never going to happen in the hardware business. There's no future here."

I had to come down anyway. I took it one step at a time. "I'm not talking about the future," I told my father. "When it comes to what's way ahead, like Technology or the Institute, I'm all for that. And the moon, too, everything that's in the future. That's fine. All I had in mind was to keep on in Serenity, and help in the store the same as always, with you. For next summer."

I waited for my father to answer.

"It's only a couple of months away," I pointed out. "No more than six or seven. You couldn't call that the future, anything so close."

"Well." My father came over and pulled the ladder into position for the next two letters, M and A. "General Magneto's nothing we have to decide right this minute. It's just a thought."

"Can't we stop thinking about it? The thought it is? Just forget it?"

He went back to the desk to get his coat. "At least, we can stop talking about it." He folded the newspaper. "I'll see you at home, Andy. I've got to drop by and speak to Ben Wolf."

"Not about General Magneto?"

"Stop worrying." He laughed. "Ben and I have a lot of paper work left over from yesterday, invoices and the rest to straighten out." He stopped by the counter. "As far as General Magneto goes, Andy, the whole thing's only a possibility. A vague possibility."

That didn't sound so bad. I watched my father go out the door. A possibility is where anything can happen, even nothing. It's not like a fact, where it's all over with and you can't do anything about it. I took my father's suggestion not to worry, too much. I put all my attention back into the thumbtacks, getting them up straight into the ceiling. The bell over the door let go again, and it was Onion John.

He was still dressed in the coat with the velvet collar and the fedora hat. He was wearing his sneakers though. I guess the other shoes were too pointed for comfort.

I came down off the ladder and we stood at the counter. Even though I understood him as well as ever, I didn't know what to talk to him about after all the changes that came out of Onion John Day. I asked him how he liked his house, the first night he spent in it. He said fine. He asked me how I liked the house.

"The blue on the ceiling," I told him, "that's pretty."

He took the strap hinges out of his pocket, the ones he bought at the beginning. He was going to ask my father if we'd take them back because he might as well get his twenty-seven cents.

"I can take care of that." I took the hinges. "Rusch's always refunds anybody's money." I took a quarter and two pennies out of the cash register and remarked, "I'm sorry they didn't work out."

It's the kind of remark you have to make when you give a refund, how sorry you are. But John didn't take it that way. He told me I didn't have to be sorry. It's true there never would have been a new house if it weren't for me, and the hinges and my father. But that was nothing for me to be sorry about. He patted my hand. He didn't think it would take very long before he got used to the place. It was going to turn out fine, once the new house got to seem more like home and not just somewhere he was visiting.

The more he tried to make me feel better, the worse I began to feel that the hinges didn't work. From the way John sounded and the way I felt, it would have been a lot better if we'd just fixed the door somehow and let it go at that. There was no use talking about it, though. I didn't say anything, once John got finished cheering me up.

He sat down on a stack of paint cans and took out his purse to put away the twenty-seven cents. Now the business part was finished I couldn't see what else we had to go into. John sat and I stood with my elbows on the glass case, and we put in the longest time we'd ever been together without John talking. After a while he took some papers out of his inside pocket and he asked how much longer I thought it would be, before my father got back.

"He's not coming back. He went over to see Mr. Wolf, the one who works down at General Magneto."

John didn't know about General Magneto and there was no use going into the possibility that was. He handed me the papers. They were left with him the night before and he wanted to ask my father about them, what they were. They were fancy looking papers with a design on the top page, where it was folded over. It was the insurance policy,

Comprehensive Liability and Workmen's Compensation.

"Compranshy?" John tried to repeat the name. He didn't know "Compranshy" was papers. He thought it was a charm, the way my father talked about it, a spell. My father never did clear up for him what insurance was. He asked me.

"It's like a bet you make," I explained. "If you have a car you bet this company, say, fifty dollars you're going to have a wreck. And if you do, then the company has to pay you what the wreck is worth, whether it's five hundred or even a thousand dollars. But if you don't, then you lose the fifty dollars you put in. That's all insurance is."

John worked one hand over his face like he was checking to see if he needed a shave. He couldn't understand, he said, why my father should want to play betting games with him. Why did Mr. Rusch say everyone was protected?

"They are in a way. If they get their back broke or they get killed, then they're protected."

John held his ears to the side of his head. The way things stood, he told me, everyone who worked on the building was doomed. He studied the floor. There had to be a way to protect the people of Serenity from accidents and plagues. After searching around on the floor, he came up with it. A goat! There had to be a special kind of house-warming, he explained, with a goat as the chief guest. The goat had to be brought into the house for what sounded like a barn dance.

The house had to be filled with friends. He asked me if I'd come up the next afternoon. Me? He wanted me to bring Eechee and Bits and Hemmendinger. Me, he asked, would I come?

"How about my Pa? Don't you want him?"

John went back to looking at the floor. He didn't think my father would like so much to see a goat in the new house. I didn't think so either. Besides, John asked, out of everybody, including my father, wasn't I his oldest friend?

"If you think of it that way," I told him, "I guess I am." It was certainly a fact. It was more of a fact than any other kind of friend. It was one you couldn't change. "If you really want me to come, I'll be glad to come."

John couldn't think of anything that was more important.

"Then I will. And I can promise you the others will come too."

John picked up speed. He told me where he was going to get the goat and all the other preparations that went into the housewarming. I leaned on my hand and listened to him, all the different words coming out of the clatter. He didn't seem so changed. Not when he let out some of the things were going to happen up at his house the next afternoon. Except by the next afternoon, it was too late to visit Onion John in his new house.

Chapter 13

A fire in Serenity starts with a call to Ollie's Diner, which is on Water Street right next to the Good Will Fire Company, No. 1. Not that there's any number two fire company, or three or four. Though someday there may be and then you'll be able to tell which was the first.

The reason you call the Diner to report a fire is someone's always there. The place is open to all hours and Ollie sleeps out back. Whereas the firehouse, usually it's locked and empty because it's volunteer and no one gets paid to sit around and play checkers or lean against it, the way I've seen them in Easton where they make a steady job of being a fireman.

So the number that's written over everyone's telephone, for an emergency, is Ollie's. When someone calls about a fire, Ollie does four things. He goes to the firehouse and hoists up the doors. He presses the button that works the alarm. He calls Dusek, Mantini and Kay. These are three farmers who live in different directions out of town, and when they hear from Ollie where the fire is they tell their neighbors so they're saved from the trip downtown. While he's on the phone, Ollie writes on a blackboard the location of the fire. That way, anyone who shows up late knows where to go.

The next thing Ollie does is only sometimes. And that is to call the *Globe* if he thinks the paper would be interested in the fire. The *Globe* pays Ollie two dollars for every fire that they print. Ollie's the only one who makes any money out of a fire in Serenity but considering all the extra work he does, for free, no one begrudges him. By the time anyone shows up Ollie already has his fire hat on and he's at the wheel of the engine and he's moving out.

Ollie was serving a truck driver his breakfast that Tuesday morning when the call came in. It was from Mr. Tracy who runs an orchard on the other side of Hessian Hill. "All I said to Tracy was 'No!'," Ollie told us. "I couldn't believe it. Good grief, a terrible thing like that was hard to believe."

Just about the time the phone was getting ready to go in Ollie's, I was on DuBrock Street on my way to school. I was figuring out in my head how many days were left until the end of June and it amounted to two hundred and seventeen days. That seemed a pretty good stretch before I had to face any vague possibilities like General Magneto. Two hundred and seventeen days in Serenity with nothing

154

to worry about and with John my oldest friend, that seemed like a lot to look forward to. I'd just picked up a leaf. It was sugar maple. There were hardly any leaves around, with any gold in them or red. And the ones were left, you noticed.

When a cow, a cow that had to be as big as a cloud, began to bawl. All of a sudden Serenity was like an empty barn with a cow in it struck down by colic. It stopped me dead. Until I remembered. It was the new alarm the Fire Department put in, instead of a siren. They called it a squawker. But the noise it made sounded like a hurt cow, big as any you can imagine, bawling.

I ran. All along DuBrock Street doors opened. Women stood. And men rushed out, fighting into their coats. From between houses, cars rolled back. They hit the street with a bump and let off downhill. The cow bawled and you could hear yells now, too. From all over. And then a regular siren came on and steadied into short blasts. It was the alarm for the ambulance corps. A bunch of kids rounded out of DePew Street, heading back from school. They pounded downhill. A lot of the yelling came from them. Eechee was at the end of the mob. He saw me and he hollered, "Who is it?"

"I don't know!" I yelled. But I did, I did know. Somehow it came when I was running, like a breath that I took. But it didn't leave, the idea, when I let go of the air that was in me and went empty and had to pull for some more.

I knew. Even before the engine went by, at the end of DuBrock Street.

Ollie was at the wheel. My father hung off the back. There were better than a dozen firemen crowding the top of the engine and hugging the sides.

"It's Onion John!" The engine flashed past. "Onion John!"

"Onion John!" It came from behind me now. From all over. "Onion John!" A couple of men stopped running. They turned back to their cars, now they knew where the fire was. The tank truck went by, down below, with its howler going. It carried even more firemen than the engine ahead. "Onion John!" was the yell you heard from anyone who looked at you.

The ambulance swept past down the hill and swayed into Water Street. By the time I came to the corner, Water Street was crowded with people running out of town. No one in his right mind would set out to run all the way to Hessian Hill, six miles! But they ran anyway because what else was there to do? I ran.

A horn honked behind me. It was Mr. Kinnoy's station wagon pulling into the curb, its door swinging open. Eech ran back to crowd in after me. The wagon was jammed.

"John's place, it's a total wreck."

"It exploded. Boom!"

"The body was thrown clear with the first blast."

I tried not to listen. Every fire you go to, you hear stories

156

on the way. The worse they are, the more attention they get. Until it's a race who can tell the most awful. But not listening, you start thinking on your own how bad it could be. I didn't know what to do, listen or think, on the way up to Hessian Hill in Mr. Kinnoy's station wagon.

He wasn't dead. He was running from the brook with a pail of water when we pulled in. Onion John wasn't even hurt.

But the whole west wall of the house was climbing with flame. And the smoke poured off the top of Hessian Hill like it was a volcano.

Across the field in back of John's house the fire engine bumped its way toward Onion John's brook, paying out hose as it went. There was a good hundred and fifty feet to go but the distance wasn't the problem. The Serenity pumper carries fifteen hundred feet of two and a half inch hose. The problem was water. There wasn't enough water in the little trough Onion John used for his house supply. By the time we got there they were damming up the stream, fifteen men with picks and shovels, so there'd be a decent pool of water to draw from.

The tank truck was in front of the house. It carries seven hundred and fifty gallons of water and its own pump, so it can start before the engine is ready to go. The first stream that came off the hose of the tank truck was solid water with Barney McSwain the lead man at the nozzle.

"No, Barney. Spread it!" Mr. Kinnoy is an ex-fire chief

and one of the best firemen in town. He grabbed the nozzle and worked a valve to one side. The solid water spread out and started to fog and Mr. Kinnoy moved in to throw a curtain of water around the west wall. It could've been gasoline, for all the good it did. The flames held high and a red cloud tore out the front door. The second hose, the one from the engine, whipped out just about then and went to work on the door. For a couple of minutes, it looked hopeless. The water poured in and the red boiled out. But after the hose from the engine moved closer, the fire bellied back from the door. In that one spot, at least, the fire turned into smoke and steam.

The crowd of us cheered, for something to do. There were almost as many as on Sunday. And except for the firemen, we could only stand. And watch the house we built burn down. It was like watching your own home go. Because everyone did have a hand in the place and was proud of it, how it was built all in one day and on schedule.

Onion John ran for the steaming front door and the crowd hushed. The men at the hose grabbed John. He fought to break away, to get into the house where it was still a furnace. They pulled Onion John back and sat him down on the running board of the tank truck.

"*Stepan*" was all I could understand when they let me through the people around Onion John. He rubbed the smears on his face blacker and blacker, breathing heavy and crying and talking all at the same time.

158

"It's his valuables," I told the others. "The picture of *Saint Stepan* and the fiddle. There's other things. He wants to get them."

They wouldn't let John go. "How'd it start?" Mr. Ries yelled from the back of the truck where he watched the pump. "Ask him what started it." The crowd pressed in, asking how it started, as if the answer were the most important thing they needed to put the fire out.

John put his face in his hands. To hear him I had to get down on my knees and I listened at his hands like they were a closed door.

"He says he started it." I looked at all the people above. "Because he's dumb like an ox. And he's thick like a rock, he says. He's the one who started it."

"But how?"

It took a little while to get. It was the stove, John told me, all white and shiny and electric. How could a stupid fool like himself live with such a stove, he asked me, so magnificent. He brought it newspapers, to light it up that morning the same as he'd been doing all his life when he started a fire. And then in his terrible bonelike head, he remembered. All he had to do was turn a switch. So he put the newspapers on the stove and turned a switch and he went off to get water for his coffee. And that wasn't all. In his dumbness, he looked out the door at the morning, at the beautiful sun and he came out to smell the fine day. When he looked back there was blood red streaking through the smoke, jumping off the stove where the newspapers had caught. The wall was on fire. John threw the water that was in his hand through the door and he ran. That's how the fire started, John explained, because he was a numbskull.

All anyone did, when I finished, was nod. The crush around John loosened up. They went back to helping with the fire. Or they went to tell those who hadn't heard how the fire started. I sat there with John, on the ground next to the running board, and I told him, "It wasn't you're a numbskull. Some of these appliances are fierce, catching on to them."

No good, John stared at a rock between his feet. No good, he rapped with his knuckles on his own forehead as if he were coming to pay himself a visit. It was no good, he said. He could spend the rest of his life trying to change, but it was no good. He couldn't. He was too dumb, too stupid, too much of an ox, a mule, a buffalo, to be like anyone else. He had tried with all his might to make himself different. It was no good. He was the same as always.

"Onion John."

He looked at me, his eyes red and almost floating, his face ragged.

"That's not so bad, you're the same as always. It was pretty good, the way you were."

He started to smile but he didn't get very far with it. He started back behind his hands. There was another cheer.

We looked past the edge of the tank truck. The fire was brought under control. Part of the shingled roof was caved in but the walls stood, dripping, and there were only sparks inside, instead of fire. The place was drenched.

John was gone. He rounded the corner of the tank truck. He headed for the house. It was a last dash to find what was left of his valuables. It was a surprise and he got away with it. None of the crew on the hose laid a hand on him as he went past. It was only after he was inside, hopping across the black and crumbling beams of the floor that Mr. Kinnoy took after him, yelling, "Onion John."

Kinnoy stopped and turned away from the house. He and the gang at the hose started running. The house sagged. There was a scream. It was a wooden board slowly being ripped. Another sag and the house caved in with a long drawn out wrench and a groan. If John made any sound you couldn't hear him in the roar. The burnt out frame of the house balanced and folded into the cellar. In seconds, John's place was nothing but a hole in the ground with broken, twisted ends of lumber sticking out of it and smoke rising and dust.

I got caught in the charge, in the shrieking and running that started from everywhere to get into that hole of black rubbish and tear it apart. There was a push and I stumbled. I got slammed and I tripped and went down. I was on my knees, scrambling up to follow the crowd when the back of my neck was caught. It was Mr. Jonah Davis up from

162

Easton because of the call Ollie made at the first alarm.

"Where is he?"

I didn't stop to answer Mr. Jonah Davis. He stayed with me and we pushed our way into the wreck, down into the smoke and the heaving bodies and the swinging arms where everyone dug and pulled to get at Onion John. My jacket caught and I tore it loose.

"Where is he?" Mr. Davis kept asking.

"No!" yelled my father. "This is no time for reporters."

"You were glad to have me here on Sunday." Mr. Davis blocked his way past my father. "And this is just as big a story. Bigger! Where is he?"

There were too many of us bellowing for the next one to get out of the way. My father, Kinnoy and some of the firemen went to work on people, getting them out of the cellar. They organized a line, grabbing junk and passing it behind them up to the people who were on top. Davis went yanking at whatever he could lay his hands on, working as wild as anyone else. Down below me, at the bottom of the twisted heap, Davis was the first person to reach Onion John.

I managed to see him through the people and Onion John turned out to be the quietest person on Hessian Hill. He sat under a blackened beam that was part of the ridge pole of the house, resting with his eyes closed, waiting. And the miracle was his face. It wasn't even scratched. It was caked with charcoal and gray with ash but without a sign of blood. He opened his eyes when Davis reached him and nodded as if to say, hello. At the sight of John everyone started to work twice as hard as before, to get the rest of the stuff off him.

Except Mr. Davis. "How are you?" he leaned over John, yelling at him. "What do you think about this?"

I didn't wait to hear what Onion John had to say, working where I could.

"English!" Mr. Davis yelled. "Can't you say something in English? Please, John! Something we can print!"

I must've been six or eight feet away but I heard the words very clear.

"I feel happy."

I stopped to turn and look at Onion John. I didn't believe what I was hearing. But what other way did John have, to give Davis what he wanted? John went ahead with it. He took a long breath and kept going.

"I feel happy and very proud."

The only stretch of clear English that Onion John knew was the speech that I taught him. He recited it now for the reporter. He spoke each word of the speech clear and separate the way we rehearsed it.

"Very proud that the people of Serenity," John spoke slowly, word by word, "have fixed me up in this fine new house."

"That's Onion John!" said Eechee Ries right behind me. "He's talking!"

164

All around as they heard Onion John for the first time, heard him so they could understand, first one then another stopped working and straightened up.

"This is a good day," said Onion John, "to give thanks."

In the surprise of hearing Onion John talk, everyone held still. It was as if a tree they were used to hearing, when the wind passed through, or the noise of a brook suddenly made sense and turned into words and the tree talked, or the brook, in a plain and simple way.

"But it is hard for me to say," Onion John took a long breath and he looked up at us, "how much I appreciate all that you've done."

Onion John could hardly move, wedged like in a vise the way he was. So he couldn't, even if he wanted to, give any of the gestures we rehearsed.

He coughed and there was blood on his chin.

Chapter 14

Everyone stayed still, where they were when the first words caught them.

"Is that all you've got to say?" asked Mr. Davis.

It was like Davis pulled a trigger, of a starting gun.

"All?" yelled Mr. Kinnoy. "Isn't that enough?"

"Out of the way, Davis!" yelled my father. "Let's get to him."

"Ease that beam," yelled Mr. Ries, "the one to the right."

"Let's get him out of here!"

The crowd went frantic again, trying to clear a way for Onion John. He saw me. Onion John rolled his head for me to come to where he was pinned under the beam. I crawled down past the legs of the ones closest to him.

"Compranshy," John whispered. It was the insurance, he told me. It was the curse, and the curse had caught up with him. There was only one way he'd be saved and John asked me to help him.

166

"Andy! Out of there!"

The only way was to go ahead with the housewarming we'd planned. The goat, John whispered, first I had to bring a goat down into the wreck and then—.

"For Heaven's sakes, Andy. Come up here!"

I didn't turn around. "He's telling me what to do."

Then when I had the goat there, Onion John coughed.

Someone picked me up. Two arms came around my belly and I was lifted clear off the ground. I couldn't move my arms and I couldn't kick loose. I was put to one side. The someone who had me was Ben Wolf. He was wearing an ambulance corps hat.

"What do you want?" I asked him. "What are you doing to me?"

"There isn't any time." Ben pushed his eyeglasses back on his nose. "We've got to get that man out of here."

I was lifted again by Mr. Kinnoy up to Mr. Maibee and then to Mr. Schwarz who was on top. As soon as they let me go, I jumped back down and my father grabbed my arm.

"He was telling me what to do!" I said.

"We know what to do."

"Not about the housewarming!"

"Housewarming? Are you insane? How much warmer d'you think this place ought to be? Get back up, Andy. Stay out of this!"

All I could do was watch them pull the wreck clear. Then

167

Dr. Wallace climbed down to examine John before he was moved. He stayed down there, Dr. Wallace did, talking to the men around him while Ben Wolf and three others from the ambulance corps got John carefully, very slowly, on to a stretcher. Dr. Wallace shook his head as he talked. And those that listened to him, those men shook their heads too. The stretcher was carried to the ambulance and Ben Wolf jumped out of the back door and rushed around to the driver's seat. The motor started.

They were taking Onion John away before I knew what to do. But my father stopped me from getting to the ambulance.

"A half a minute!" I asked my father. "So he tells me what to do with the goat."

"This is no time for goats." My father sat on his heels in front of me and he held on to my shoulders. "This may be very serious. There's a cracked rib, on his left side. That's not so bad. But Dr. Wallace is afraid of the cough and the blood, he's afraid of a punctured lung."

"But John knows what to do for himself!"

"There's nothing to do until he's X-rayed."

The ambulance carefully bumped its way out of John's place and settled into the smooth road.

"A punctured lung, Andy," my father tightened the grip he had, "can be fatal. Often it is. We can hope, that's all, the X-ray shows that the lung is all right. There's nothing else we can do."

The ambulance took on speed and the dust from it waved a slow goodbye over Hessian Hill. I looked down to where I'd torn the pocket of my mackinaw away. It was hanging and I folded the cloth back on itself so the look of it was neater. Maybe on account of the fire I hadn't noticed how frosty the morning was, the chill. I buttoned my coat while my father watched. He buttoned the top button.

"If there's any chance of fatal," I asked my father, "then oughtn't we try everything. Even a goat?"

"What we ought to try for," he lifted my chin, "is self-control. All of us." He looked my face over. I felt all right, as far as control went. A couple of breaths came choppy, until I let go all the way and then hauled in. It went smooth from then on.

"The best thing you can do for the next couple of hours," my father said, "is get back to school. The lot of you. To get your mind going on something."

Back in the seat I had in class near the window, after the cars brought us down from Hessian Hill, I got my mind going on *3x over 8 plus 2 equals 11*. That's the problem we were given to solve. I didn't get very far with it. If it was going to be fatal with John, fatal meant dead. So why was I trying to find out what *x* equals? The *x*'s and *pluses* that covered my paper, all they amounted to was something like the picture of a cemetery. I drew a goat, instead. I put eyeglasses on him, the sort Ben Wolf wears. And the goat turned out to be a very smart looking animal. A smart goat, once I brought him up to John's place, might know what to do by himself.

At least, getting a goat up there, that'd be something along the lines of what John had in mind. At least, there was a chance with a goat where with *3x over 8 plus 2 equals 11*, there was no chance at all.

I tore up the sheet of paper into four small parts. On the back of each little square I wrote the word, *Hemarzrich*. It was the first time since Halloween anyone of us had used the secret code that meant the others had to help. I passed the notes along to Ries and Hemmendinger and Schwarz. Then I raised my hand to be excused.

Eechee was the first one after me, into the BOYS. Schwarz showed up with a handful of pencils he was supposed to sharpen. By the time Bo made it, I was already explaining how for land sakes alive we had to get out of there, out of school and back to Hessian Hill and hold the housewarming ourselves.

"How?" asked Bitsy. "What do we do with the goat?"

"I don't know. We'll have to see. But just sitting around here, that could be fatal for Onion John. And it'll be on our heads. On us."

"Why?" asked Bo. "Why's it our heads?"

"All it is," said Eech, "it's a terrible accident."

"It's no accident. It was the stove! They never should've put one in."

"Then why's it us?" said Bo. "It's the town's, your

170

father and everybody; it was their fault putting in the new stove."

"It wasn't them." I shook my head. "Everybody and my father were doing the best they knew how for Onion John."

"Then why's it our fault? Us?" asked Eech.

"I guess it isn't." I looked around to one of the wash bowls and turned on the hot water. The faucet works on a spring so that water only runs when you hold it. I spurted the water a couple of times before I made up my mind to tell them who's fault it was. "If you heard John, the speech he made when he thanked everybody?"

They nodded.

"The one he had most to thank was me." I held the water till it steamed. "When it comes down to anybody, it was my fault. If I wasn't John's oldest friend, the one who understood him, my father wouldn't ever have gone up there to Hessian Hill. That's so and it was even in the paper there wouldn't be any new house, if not for me. So that's whose fault it is. And when I say we got to do something. I mean me. And you have to help." I couldn't stand around all day waiting for them to answer. "Why are you looking at me like I was crazy?"

"I'm ready to help." Eech took a twist out of one of the faucets. "Except who're you to take the blame for everything?"

"Because I am, that's all. John said so himself. There's no point talking about blame. You can forget it. And you can forget about *Hemarzrich*, too, if you want. If that's the way the three of you feel, then what's the use of talking?"

"What're you getting sore about?" Eech let go of the faucet. "I said I was ready to help."

"Just because I asked what to do with the goat," Bitsy explained, "that doesn't mean I'm not ready, does it?"

"Me too!" said Bo.

I didn't know what there was I could do, but at least I had help. At least, we were on our way. The three of them followed me. To get out of school we took a chance on the front door instead of the basement, because the janitor's usually somewhere around down there. The stairs weren't any problem, we took them two at a time. It was the front hall, past the principal's office, we had to look out for.

We handled it like we were on TV, sliding along the walls and ducking past the doors, under where the glass was. We made it to the big main door without anyone seeing us. Except it wasn't necessary to sneak out of school. The lunch bell sounded. All we had to do was straighten up and walk out the big main door, with a flood of first and second graders tearing around us.

And even getting up to Hessian Hill, that wasn't necessary. From the back way we were taking out of town, we looked down an alley to the hardware store and there were a lot of cars parked in front. Including the ambulance.

"Wolf's back." Eech pointed. "He'd know, wouldn't he?

What happened at the hospital? How Onion John is?"

We headed down the alley and the closer we came to the hardware store, the better it looked. Through the windows we could see the store was crowded and we could see the men laughing. And no more than we opened the door, my father shouted, "It's okay, Andy. He's out of danger! Onion John is all right!"

Eech yipped. He and Bo and Bitsy went charging into the bunch around Ben Wolf who had all the news. I closed the door behind me and leaned against it until the bell up top stopped jangling. The hardware store is always worth smelling when you come in, a little sweet and oily and old. I took time for self-control, too, with my back and different joints and in my knees.

He was all right and I could take the time now. Even if everything that did happen was my fault, at least none of it was fatal. And when you stopped for a second, to think, John's new house wasn't my fault either, not anymore. Now that it was gone. Onion John could go back to living the way he wanted to. Except for his valuables, *Stepan* and the fiddle. They were my fault. But a picture of an old saint, anyone good at drawing could work that out. And there were plenty of old fiddles around and Rusch's stocked friction tape, all we'd need. When you came to look at it the fire might be the best thing could've happened to John as long as the rest of him was okay.

And from the way Ben Wolf talked, there didn't seem

173

to be any question of that. "They had John in a bath when I left," he said. "The nurse figured it would take two or three hours soaking to get through to him. What with the fire and just generally."

"But they're sure about it?" I pushed through to my father. "The X-ray?"

"His lung wasn't touched." Ben Wolf answered me.

"And the rib isn't so bad?" I asked my father.

"It's strapped," Ben answered me again. "It'll heal in no time."

"How long," I asked my father, "before they let John come back?"

"Why don't you ask Ben Wolf?" said my father. "He's the one who was there."

It was just I didn't feel like talking to Ben Wolf, right then. He was part of what no one had to think about for months to come, not until next summer. It was Eech told me that the hospital was going to keep John for about a week, to observe him.

"So it's all off," said Bitsy. "No use messing around with a goat now, is there?"

"What goat?" asked Ernie Miller, from the *Lamp*, behind me.

"Yes," said my father. "What was that all about, Andy, in the middle of everything?"

"John thought a goat would help him." I told about John's plans for the housewarming. "He couldn't see any

174

use you get out of being protected with Compranshy. That's the insurance, he meant. You know, Comprehensive."

"He couldn't see any use?" My father shook his head. A couple of men laughed and my father laughed too. "It's only a life saver that's all it is. If it weren't for that policy we'd never be able to rebuild his house."

"What house?"

"John's new house."

Eechee looked at me. And so did Bo Hemmendinger and Bitsy Schwarz. "You're going to rebuild the whole house? That is, the same as it was?" I asked my father.

"Of course, Andy. That's the good of insurance. John's not going to lose out just because of the fire. We're putting him right back into it, the identical place, nail for nail."

"But you can't," I told my father.

"Can't what?"

"You can't do that. The thing is, you can't do that to me. I was lucky enough it wasn't fatal for Onion John. But a whole new house, that would be my fault too. Anything that happens, I'd be the one to blame."

"What's all this about you?" asked my father. "We're concerned with Onion John, getting a home for him. A proper place for Onion John to live in."

"But he can't live that way. He says it's no use trying. Wouldn't it be just as good, as far as Onion John goes, to leave him alone?"

175

My father started to smile at me, shaking his head. But when Ernie Miller from the *Lamp* interrupted, my father seemed to forget what he was going to say to me. He stopped smiling, too.

"The boy's right," said Ernie. "I think we've done enough for Onion John."

My father lifted up from leaning on the counter. He went up straight and his arms crossed. He held his elbows. The others around quieted too, looking at Ernie.

"Hasn't it become pretty obvious?" asked Ernie. "What we think is proper and what John thinks is proper, they're two different things. What are we trying to prove to him, that he's wrong?"

"Now, Ernie. We went all through this with you at the first Rotary meeting." My father waited until a couple of men nodded. "We're not going to rehash that discussion all over again. Not now."

"A lot's happened. We almost killed the man, doing him good. I think he's had it. I think we ought to forget the new house."

"That's what I think," I told my father.

"Not now, Andy. We'll go into this later." My father came out from behind the counter until I couldn't see his face anymore, the way he stood facing Mr. Miller. "This town took on an obligation, Ernie. To Onion John. And to ourselves. We've had a setback. All right. We didn't look for this to happen, but we're not going to let it stop us."

"We'd look foolish," said Mr. Ries, "backing out now."

"Onion John's our responsibility," said my father. "We decided to help him. And he needs our help more, right now, than he ever did before."

Most everybody agreed with my father. It came to sound like politics. Democracy came into it, which is what you hear about when there's going to be a vote or an election. Ernie said that no one's private rights ought to get invaded even if it's with kindness. And my father said that democracy didn't mean we ought to leave the next fellow go hang and not care how he got along. It went too fast for me to follow, and too loud. Judge Brandstetter said the question ought to be argued out in a regular way by the town council because Onion John had become a town matter by then. They all agreed, there ought to be a meeting. But it went on anyway, Ernie and my father and Ries and Brandstetter and Wolf and the crowd of them.

I left. Even though a good stiff argument with a lot of men lambasting each other can lead almost anywhere. And usually it's worthwhile staying around to watch what develops.

But this time I thought I might as well leave. My father said we'd go into it later, anyway. And now that I was going back to school, after all it was my lunch hour. And this time, besides all that, for the first time in my life I wasn't on my father's side. So there wasn't much use in sticking around.

Chapter 15

But it certainly didn't mean I had to run away from home. Just because we weren't on the same side together, me and my father.

All the running away I ever thought about was when I wanted to join the Third Cavalry Detachment in Fort Laramie and practiced drumming until I found there wasn't any more cavalry. Or any Fort Laramie either, except it's a town in Kansas. And of course, pirates. I put in a couple of days thinking I ought to ship out for one of those. But all that was when I was six. I haven't had any of those ideas since.

So it wasn't as if I was looking for an excuse to leave town, my father and mother and Serenity for good. It was just that there didn't seem to be any other chance for me to help Onion John.

I couldn't let him be moved back into a completely rebuilt new house. Where anything that happened would be my fault. And I couldn't side with Ernie Miller. Because how would I feel if I got into an argument with George Connors, who usually ends up sitting on your head when he argues. And my father came along? And he sided with George? I'd feel awful. It was bad enough I couldn't be on my father's side. I couldn't go lining up with Ernie Miller against him.

Especially after what Ernie wrote in the *Lamp*. In the paper he put out Wednesday, because Thursday was Thanksgiving, you could see he was talking about my father. "Let our knights in shining hardware spare Onion John," it said, "not spear him with their good intentions." Seeing how Rusch's is the only hardware store in Serenity, my father had every reason to take that personally. He put in the whole week end winding up to get back at Ernie. By talking to people about the council meeting that was coming, until it looked like everybody was going to vote with my father. And by writing the speech he was going to make.

My mother and I heard the speech right through the week end, in bits and pieces as my father made it up. And at breakfast on Monday we heard the whole thing through. By then, it sounded fine. Except it was just the opposite of what I wished my father was saying.

My mother applauded and I couldn't help but join in, to show how good the speech was. "That new gesture," she said, "where you clench your fist with your thumb up," she

179

jabbed away as if she were ringing a doorbell. "That looks stunning."

"I didn't even realize I was doing it." My father was pleased. "It came out of the way I feel, I guess." He squared up the papers he had. "Anyway, I'm all set for tomorrow night."

There wasn't much time left if ever I was going to help Onion John. When my father finished his coffee, he looked at me and he asked, "How about it, Andy, does the speech convince you?" I figured the time had come when I ought to go into it, to do what I could.

"It certainly does," I said. "I don't see how Ernie Miller's going to argue against a speech like that."

"Well, I'm glad you're convinced. After what you said down at the hardware store."

"Me? I wasn't trying to argue with you, not like Ernie Miller. All I want to do is ask you a favor."

"What?"

"I want to ask you please not to build Onion John a new house again."

My father waited for whatever else I had in mind. There was nothing else I wanted except to ask him the favor. He picked up his speech from the table. "Didn't you hear any of this?" It was quiet the way he spoke. "The reasons why we're going ahead."

"I think they're fine," I told him. "All those reasons. Except Onion John doesn't want any new house."

180

My father nodded seriously when I told him that. He thought it over, squaring up the papers again on the table. He looked at my mother drinking her coffee and then he laid the speech down carefully, so the papers stayed neat. "Maybe you're right, Andy. Maybe Onion John doesn't want a new house."

"Then why build it up again?"

"Take you," said my father.

"Me?" I couldn't see why he was changing the subject so fast. "I wanted to talk about Onion John."

"You're the one who's important here," said my father. "And tell me, Andy, how much did you know a year ago about some of the plans we've been talking about? The things you're going to do?"

"Like the Institute? The way we've been talking about Technology? What've they got to do with Onion John?"

With only one day left to get John settled, I didn't see why we were talking about what didn't have to happen for years yet, to me.

"It all fits in, Andy. You couldn't have made any of those plans by yourself. You didn't know enough. Those were matters too strange and too new for you to even think about. And maybe the whole idea didn't sound too good to begin with. But as time goes by, you're beginning to see the possibilities there are, the kind of life it'll be. Isn't that so?"

"Well, I understand a lot more about it, sure."

"And the chances are, a dozen years from now, you'll thank your lucky stars for the career you're in. But no matter how far you go, Andy, the start was something you couldn't decide for yourself. You wouldn't know how to go about it. Someone had to make up your mind for you, what you wanted to do and how to live. And it's the same with Onion John."

I was glad we were back to Onion John and I nodded.

"He doesn't know what it means to live decently. All we're doing is to give him the chance to find out. He'd never know if he kept on living the way he was. And if he's a little unhappy at the start, well, that's part of it, part of getting used to a new idea. It's no more than the gripe you might feel, first off, about putting in next summer down at General Magneto."

I felt like a drink. Not milk, because there was a pitcher of that on the table. I felt like a glass of water. And I went over to the sink to get it.

But even at the faucet, with my back to my father so that I didn't have to look at him, I couldn't decide what my father was trying to say about General Magneto. I could see about Onion John. It was clear, it was very clear I wasn't helping him to get left alone. But me and General Magneto, that sounded like it was all settled too. Except the last time we talked there were two hundred and seventeen days before anyone had to think about General Magneto. And all those days I had to look forward to, they couldn't

182

come to an end right this morning. I was pretty sure my father wasn't trying to say anything like that. But I thought I'd better stop drinking water and find out.

"It's not the same, is it?" I held on to my glass. "Because Ben Wolf and General Magneto are vague. After all, they're no more than possibilities to think over."

"No." My father shook his head at me when I turned. "I asked Ben to fix it. And he has." There wasn't any more doubt about what my father was trying to say. He just said it. "It's all arranged. There's a job waiting for you at General Magneto. That's what you're going to do. Why waste another summer down at the hardware store?"

I didn't answer him right off. Because that's when the thought struck me. How there was one more, last way that I could help Onion John. It came to me right out of the blue and I went back to drinking water. I could run away with Onion John. It was a surprise, even to me, how simple the idea was. But before I put my mind to it, I wanted to make sure.

"It's all arranged?" I sounded hollow from talking into the glass.

My father shook his head, once, to say yes. "Ben's set up an interview down there and I thought one of these days—"

My mother interrupted. "Andrew," she told my father, "you'd better get going. It's late."

According to the alarm clock on the window sill above the sink it wasn't so late. But my mother insisted. "We've gone far enough, Andrew, for the moment. It's late. We can leave this for some other time."

My father took another look at the clock and remembered he had to be down at the store early. "See you, Andy," he said. I nodded to him as he left the kitchen, without talking, because the glass was clamped between my teeth. And besides my new idea was spreading out and I was beginning to see how good it was. Why it never came into my head before, that's the only part I couldn't figure.

"What's the idea of all the water?" my mother asked me. "If you're thirsty, sit down and have some milk."

I got the glass from between my teeth. And I sat down. It was absolutely clear. If they couldn't leave Onion John alone, my father and the town, then what was more natural. Onion John could leave them alone. If he wanted to stay the way he was, John's only chance was somewhere else. It was that simple.

"Andy," said my mother.

"Yes ma'am."

"I want you to understand your father."

"There's nothing so hard about it. Onion John's going to get built up again. And I'm going down to General Magneto."

"Let's leave Onion John out of this. It's your Pa I want you to understand, the plans he's making for you."

There was nothing else to think about, for me, except Onion John. The idea was only the beginning. To get set to run away, there's a lot to decide on. For instance, how soon? And then, where to?

"It might help you to know this, Andy. There's one thing your father's never told you about your career. It's a lot older than you are. It used to belong to him."

And a third was, what to take along?

"Andy."

"I'm listening."

"Does it help you to understand, that your father wanted to be an engineer? It was radio in his time. But all the plans he has for you, those were the things he was going to do himself. He was going to leave Serenity. And he was going up to M. I. T. And on, from there. That used to be his career, Andy."

"What happened?"

"Well, there were circumstances. And you happened, you were one of them. Anyway, he never made it. But your father held to that plan, he's kept it bright and new with the thought he's put into it year after year. And now he's giving it to you. You mightn't think much of it, at the moment. But no matter how you feel about that career, Andy, I want you to remember it's about the most valuable possession your father has."

"I'll remember," I said.

My mother made a pile out of three or four dishes. She started to collect the silverware too and had a fistful before she stopped.

"Not only remember it. But consider it. Try to understand how your father feels about it."

"I'll try." I figured we'd have a lot of time once we left town to consider how my father wanted to be an engineer. South was where we'd probably head, now it was December. Out in the desert or under a palm tree, we'd have plenty of time. "I'll certainly try," I told her.

"Andy!" It was Eechee Ries outside, come to pick me up on the way to school. He banged at the door and opened it. He stared at me, surprised, as if I'd already told him what I was going to do. "Wait'll you hear!" he said.

"Wait'll you hear!" I told him. I could just see Ries keel over when he heard I was going to run away.

"Onion John's gone," said Eech. "He's skipped the hospital. He's run away."

"By himself?" I asked.

"Yes," said Eech.

Chapter 16

The door closed. Eech bumped it with his backside and it closed.

There wasn't much more he had to tell us about Onion John running away. Just that he did. Ben Wolf heard the report from the hospital that Onion John's bed wasn't even slept in. Eech heard it from Mr. Kinnoy, not two minutes before, just around the corner. For all the questions my mother asked, that's all there was to find out. Onion John had run away. That was enough, it seemed to me, and I listened without asking any questions.

I listened and I looked at the door behind Eech. It has four panels, the door in our kitchen, two long ones at the bottom and square ones on top. It has an Erwin lock that's mortised in, not screwed on the outside, and a pair of heavy brass knobs. The door has a nice balance to it. One touch and it closes solid with a loud click when the latch springs home.

The door's been around as long as I have. But I never

came to notice all the things about it the way I did that morning. And the reason is, that's how I felt when Eech said, "He's run away!" Like a door closed. And watching a real door actually close, a second later, I suppose that's what made me notice.

I saw I couldn't leave Serenity, not with Onion John. Because he was gone. And I couldn't stay, not with my father. Because I was on my way to General Magneto. And in four more years I was on my way out of Serenity for good. Both ways, it was like a door closed.

And there was nothing to do, nothing at all, except to go to school and study about World War I in history. And *Ivanhoe* in English. And the isosceles triangle. And in geography, Brazil, its resources. I found out about Woodrow Wilson, all his problems. And about knights with their battle axes. And 130 degree angles. And the coffee bean. But I didn't find out how it happened with me. How it ever happened that anyone could start out with as good a friend as Onion John, and as good a father as the one I had, and end up nowhere. Behind a closed door.

The only decent thing about that Monday was the kind of day it was. If you felt mean and miserable and hopeless. it was a great day for that. It was cold and gray and the damp cut into you, and it felt like snow. It was a great day to go no place but home and to stay behind closed doors. But I didn't go home from school. On account of Eech, again.

He has ears like an elephant. Whatever's going around, he's likely to hear it soon. Like that morning, how Onion John had run away. And that afternoon, how Onion John was seen up on Hessian Hill digging in his garden. It was Mr. Tracy who saw him. When Tracy yelled, Onion John dropped what he was doing and headed for the woods. A car, full of men, had gone up to Hessian Hill to find John and take him back to the hospital. Eech heard it all from the janitor, down in the basement during afternoon recess.

It was a hope. It meant that Onion John hadn't lit out for west of the Rockies, somewhere. It could mean he was still around.

"We could be the ones to find him," I told Eech. "Instead of whoever it was that went up to Hessian Hill."

"What for? To send him back to the hospital?"

"No." I didn't want to let Eech in on my plan to run away with John. "Maybe we could help him stay out of sight. They might vote different at the meeting tomorrow night, if they think John's gone. Besides," I told Eech, "*Hemarzrich.*"

"Sure," said Eech. "I'm ready to go look."

Hessian Hill's to the east of Serenity. There was no use going there, long as the place was covered. We headed west. We knew most of John's favorite spots on the Musconetty and we checked down the creek until we came to Mantini's meadows where we cut across to look along the big river. It was Eech who thought of McKardle's cave.

This isn't a real cave, just an old foundation dug into a slope high over the river, in back of where the Duseks farmed. Part of it was covered over, so you could think of it as a cave, and John talked of the place as ideal to settle in for anyone who was looking around. We hauled ourselves up there.

The day it was, you didn't know whether it was over with and night was coming or whether it was hours yet until supper. Either way, McKardle's cave was the last chance we had. We couldn't make any time wading up through the fallen leaves, pulling ourselves past the wet empty trees and climbing over one ledge of stone then another. If there was nothing to see in McKardle's cave, all we had left was to head back to town.

He was there! When we came over the crest of the hill and looked down the river side to the cave below, there sat Onion John in front of a little fire.

All he had on was a nightgown, a hospital nightgown for a shirt and a pair of pants pulled over it. But to me he looked better than I ever saw him in all my life. He looked wonderful.

"Onion John!" Eech and I didn't care if they heard us back in Serenity. We jumped and we landed on the floor of the foundation in a dead heat, the two of us.

John jumped too. He headed straight out of sight. He disappeared behind the stone wall that was part of the old cellar.

"John!" I yelled. "It's only us. It's me, Andy. And Eechee Ries."

John peeked back around the edge of the stone.

"Only us!"

John made the trip back as fast as he left. He came down to his knees and threw an arm around Eech and one around me, like we were a couple of ball carriers he was tackling. We yelled at the squeeze he put on.

"You look great," I told him. "How do you feel?"

John let go and he moaned. The trouble was he felt fine. His rib and all the rest of him was just fine. And still they insisted on keeping him in the hospital. All they did was bathe him, he complained, once every day. That was one of the reasons he ran away, to escape from all the baths. Another reason was to get to his garden before the cold froze it solid, so he could spade it up for a winter crop of rye. But the big reason was the meeting. He'd heard they were going to vote him back into the new house.

"It's practically certain," I told Onion John. "Especially after they hear my father's speech. It convinced me."

John nodded. That's what he was afraid of, and sitting in a tub of hot water there was nothing he could do about it. But now he was out he certainly didn't intend to let the house be voted up again.

"Don't you worry," I told him. "I know how to stop them. A plain, easy, simple way."

John wasn't worried. He had plans of his own, to keep

them from building any more houses. He brought us over to the fire to listen.

And then he came out with the most ridiculous, the dog-awfulest notion I ever heard of. He said he was going to fumigate the whole town of Serenity, just the way he smoked the evil spirits out of my cellar on Halloween eve. John had the idea that if he collected a pile of oak and got a fire started with a twirling stick when the wind was in the right direction, that would solve his problem. He actually believed that if the people around town breathed in the smoke, it would get rid of the evil spirits that were in them.

He went on that way, explaining it all as if it were the most sensible idea in the world. He said it was the evil spirits in the people of Serenity that plagued them into building the new house. And he was positive, once the smoke drifted through the town it would carry the evil spirits away. And then everyone would forget about the vote. And they'd all go back to being ordinary good friends of his again, with no more on their mind than to wish him, "Good day."

"Onion John," I said when he finished and stood by the fire smiling at Eechee and me, "if you ask me, that's not such a good idea. I don't think it'll get you anywhere."

John stood there a little bewildered, pleased as he was with the plan he figured out.

"There's only one way you're going to stop them," I

said. "Only one, sure, practical way. And that is, you've got to leave town. You have got to run away from Serenity."

John leaned way back with his palms out. He couldn't see that at all. He liked Serenity. He shook his head. Why should he run away?

"It doesn't look as if they're ever going to leave you alone, John. So, you've got to leave them alone. It's the only way!"

John picked up a branch from a pile of wood he'd gathered. He broke it over his knee and he tossed the pieces on the fire. Onion John asked me to please explain to him what was wrong with the oak fire, the notion he had.

"It won't work." I didn't just want to tell him how mixed-up and far-fetched it was. I thought I'd prove it to him. "When you say evil spirits, there's none of those in Serenity. Those people, they're filled with good spirits. Look, John, they want to do the best they can for you. There's no evil spirits in that. Every one of them is out to make you happy. And if you fill them with smoke that's meant for evil spirits, then no one's going to notice it. Except to sneeze, maybe."

John smiled to quiet me down. He had a theory. It was just about as sensible as the rest of it. He told how a spirit gets into a person, sometimes, hiding behind a thought that's very nice, and gentle and kind. But once inside the spirit turns out to be evil the way a crock of milk goes sour

194

on an August afternoon. He was sure that's what happened in Serenity, to everybody. What started out nice ended up, without anyone knowing, bad.

I gave up. "Onion John, what's the use arguing." This was real, the trouble he was in, and he couldn't go playing around with it like it was a fairy tale. "Trying to fumigate the evil spirits out of Serenity is just plain foolish. And that's all it is, foolish."

Onion John worked it around a couple of times, his lips moving, and then he got the word out. "Foolish?" He sat down at the fire and looked across at me, as if to check whether he had it right. He made it again, very clear. "Foolish?"

"I mean impractical." I got down on my hands and knees across from where he sat. "There's no logic to it. No rhyme or reason! Ask Eechee."

John looked behind him, to Eech. Eech sat down and picked up a piece of wood to juggle. "I don't know," he said. "It sounds just as good as a lot of other ideas that Onion John's had."

"But Eechee!" I had to get them to listen very carefully. "And John!" I waved away the smoke from between us. "This is serious, a serious situation. It's nothing you can take a chance on. And the oak fire, let's just say that it can work. For the sake of argument, let's say that. But maybe it won't work! Maybe John drowns this whole valley in smoke and still and all, the first time anyone sees him, klunk, in he goes to the hospital and up goes the house. That can happen, couldn't it?"

"Of course," said Eech. "It's possible. It could happen."

"But if he runs away, it can't happen. That's the difference. Nothing like that's possible. It just isn't!"

Eech hefted the stick in his hand. "I see what you mean." Onion John sat studying the fire, quiet as ever.

"It stands to reason, they'll never build that house for Onion John if he's not around to build it for."

Onion John left off with the fire and took to studying me. I could see he was getting the drift of it now.

"That's all I want to point out. One way's sure. There's sense to it. It can't help but work. And the other way is only maybe."

"And between the two," Eech used his stick for a poker, "I think you're right. Your way is sure."

John nodded. He held his hands out to the fire and bathed his face in the warmth he collected. When he started to talk, it was in low gear, not pushing sixty the way he usually went. My way was sure, he agreed. Except, he shrugged, he didn't want to leave Serenity. And even if his idea wasn't so sure, maybe it would root a lot of evil spirits out of the town. Maybe his way, everyone would be better off.

"Well, I don't know." I looked at the fire and Eech shifted a stick where the draft was blocked. The spot blazed up. "It's up to you to decide, Onion John. Whether you want to fix up the town or get yourself saved. It seems to me you're the one's most in trouble. And if you want to get out of it, well, you have to get out. That's about it!"

John took a long time to make up his mind. I watched him and then I watched the smoke from the fire go up, to stop and dip and circle up again until it spread into nothing, a part of the heavy gray day that was ending.

The first part of what Onion John had to say was in his own language and it sounded like the longest string of slow riding cuss words I ever heard. And then it turned out he was agreeing with me. My way was sure. It was sensible. It was the only thing he could do.

"He's going to run away, Eech!" I was on my feet looking down at them. "He's going to do it!"

"Are you, John?" asked Eech. Slowly, John nodded.

"And now!" I walked around the fire. "Wait'll you hear!"

"Something else?" Eech followed me, with his eyes.

"Maybe the best part. I didn't have in mind, John, to see you go off by yourself. On your own. Do you know what I'm going to do?" I let them wait for a couple of seconds to find out what I was smiling at. "I'm going to run away with you."

"Who?" asked Eech.

"Me."

"Why?"

"John's my fault, isn't he? Wasn't I the one had to help

him? I've had it ever since this morning, how I could. I'm going to help him run away. Do you understand, John? I'm going with you!"

The least I thought he'd be was pleased. John didn't move. As if he didn't even hear me. He sat and watched the fire. I told him again, I was going to help him. He started to shake his head. Then a rumble came out and soon he was breaking his own speed limit. It all ended up, No! He wasn't going to let me help him. And why? Because that's how all the trouble started, the help that was piled on to him. He wasn't going to take any more help. From no one. Not even me. He saw he had to run away. It was the only sure thing. But he was going by himself. Without any help.

He threw a knot of wood into the flame and the fire scattered.

"But, John," I started. "The thing is—"

And right then and there I stopped. I stopped lying. Because I could see that's all it was. Me wanting to help John run away, that was a lie. If all I wanted was for John to run away, I would've cheered that morning when Eech came through the door. When I heard John was gone. And I didn't cheer. I didn't even feel happy about it. I felt sad. A good many lies, there's at least two sides to them and you can take a point of view. But this was a flat lie. You couldn't get around it.

I sat down and I told him the honest truth. "If you want to know, John, I'm in the same fix you are. And when it comes to any help, the truth is I'm asking you to help me. For you to please let me go away with you."

"Why?" Eech was shocked. "What's the matter with you, Andy?"

"Nothing, except I'd like to stay in Serenity."

"That's why you want to run away? Where's the sense to it?"

"It's not a question what I want. I'd just as soon stay on here, down at the store, with my father. But I can't. I have to go. And I'd rather go with John, if he'll only let me, than down to General Magneto." I told them all about it, how it was settled for next summer. And then how I was going up to Technology and up to the moon, for all I knew, before I stopped going. "Unless it's okay to go with you, John."

The look of disgust came over John's face, you'd think he bit into a mildewed onion. He told me to stop lying.

"But I have. Didn't you hear, I want you to help me. That's no lie! What I'm telling you now is the absolute truth."

Not about the moon, John shook his head. There couldn't be any truth in that. Whoever heard of any one going to the moon, he asked, least of all me?

"But it is true," said Eech. "That part."

"In only a couple of years, John. There's men going to the moon. Ask anybody!"

It took us a while before John would even listen. Eech

remembered about orbits and intercontinental ballistic missiles. And I remembered about LOX, the fuel they use in rockets, and twenty-four thousand miles an hour. But it was impossible to get John to believe in a simple, ordinary, everyday fact. It was only when we swore on the name of *Stepan,* the saint from his hometown, that he began to put any trust in us. We swore three times and then he believed us.

It veered his attitude into a complete about face. He took me by the arm and held it tight. He patted me on the shoulder. I was in worse trouble, he said, than anything was happening to him. Worse trouble than anyone he ever heard about, as far back in history as he could remember.

"Then look, John, can I go with you?"

Onion John said yes.

I shot up to my feet.

"You're going?" yelled Eech. "Really, Andy?"

"We're on our way!" I swung at Eech and he belted me, harder than he had to for a celebration. I let him have one just as hard. He pushed and I sprawled, clipping him in back of the knees so he went down too. We ended up on the other side of the fire. When we looked around to John, there wasn't much of a smile on his face. He sat there quiet.

"When are you taking off?" asked Eech.

John looked up beyond the trees, studying the sky and sniffing at it. It was going to snow. But snow or not, John thought, we'd better leave that night. To put an end to anyone looking for him. And the snow wasn't so bad. When he came to Serenity, twenty-five years before, it snowed. And he'd just as soon go out of Serenity the way he came in. It was suitable, he thought. If I could get ready—

There wasn't much I needed. John was the problem, getting him outfitted. That's when *Hemarzrich* turned out to be such a good code, again. Eech promised to rustle up a couple of overcoats for John and bring them up to McKardle's cave with whatever other clothes he could lay his hands on. The food and groceries were left up to me.

"It won't take long to get ready," I said. "Except I'll have to wait until we're all asleep in our house."

"Midnight," said Eech. "That's when you ought to leave. You could meet behind the piano factory at midnight."

"Why then?"

"Think of the way it sounds. When I tell the story how the two of you left Serenity, I can say—they left at midnight."

John didn't have any objections to midnight. And neither did I. As long as it gave Eech a better story to tell. John and I shook hands. There was a wet spot on my cheek, a flake of snow. It was starting. "Midnight," I said. "Behind the piano factory."

Chapter 17

My mother looks like a very beautiful woman. She has a round face and a nose that's undersized and straight back shiny hair that rolls together behind her neck. She's not the kind of beautiful you see on TV. There's a picture we have of a beautiful woman down at the hardware store, inside the cover of a cigar box where we keep off-standard screws and nuts. My mother is beautiful the way that picture is.

I checked her over at supper that night. And my father too. I hadn't much of a chance to study either one since that morning when I decided to run away. And supper was getting close to the last chance for a good look. I could see there was nothing wrong with my father's ears. He jokes about the way they stick out. They're pretty good looking ears as far as I'm concerned. Everything else on my father's face is long, his nose and his chin and his eyebrows, the way they close in on each other.

All through the thick pea soup that was made out of the

carcass of the Thanksgiving turkey, with dumplings in it, I had the view of them pretty much to myself. Most of that time they put in on Onion John, without any need for me to join in. They wondered where he might be. My father was one of those who went up to scour Hessian Hill, and he thought it was terrible that Onion John had disappeared. He and my mother wondered how it would affect the council meeting the next night. Or whether there'd be any meeting at all. My mother had a string of pearl beads on and my father, a bow tie. The sight they made across the table, I knew I'd never forget it no matter how far away I went.

I had an extra plate of the thick pea soup. Besides being a favorite of mine, there was no way of telling how lucky we'd be getting a hitch out of town and when we'd hit a diner to get something hot. It was going to be a long night, with the wind coming up and the snow. I reminded myself how that was something I had to take along, something hot, in a thermos.

I stayed on at the dining room table with my school books and, to be sure I remembered everything, I worked on a list of what I had to take. The two went on to the living room where my mother was embroidering a pillow slip and they watched a quiz program. There was a question came up about Woodrow Wilson I knew the answer to myself. Only the lady on the program got a hundred and twenty eight thousand dollars for it.

On my own, I had a dollar and a half saved. It wasn't

much to run away on. But John had his pocketbook. And there was the snow. It made traveling worse but the snow was something to shovel to bring in a little extra.

After the quiz I heard them talk over about the late show, whether it was worth losing any sleep over. For a second I was worried because that'd keep them up until twelve thirty. My mother thought it wasn't worth going back twenty years, just to look at a picture. So the set went off. I put away my school books, in the broom closet where they'd be out of the way from now on.

I was the first one up and I was in the bottoms of my pajamas when they came to the top of the stairs. Ordinarily I yell out, but this time I went into the hall special to say good night. It was for the last time. I would've liked to say something more than usual, the occasion it was. But there's not too many different ways of saying good night, without raising suspicion. We said, "Good night, sleep tight," same as always and I went back into my bedroom and got dressed again.

I had an hour and a half to get ready.

I worked with a flashlight, picking out the clothes to put in the knapsack I had. Keeping quiet, working with that small circle of light, my breath grew shorter and shorter until I found it was stopped all together. I sat down on the bed and reasoned there was nothing to get winded about. As long as I kept very quiet. I didn't take many clothes. And there was nothing else out of my bedroom, to go, except that copy of the *Lamp* from the summer with the picture of the ball team in it.

I needed all the room there was in the knapsack for food. I found a lot of turkey wrapped in wax paper in the refrigerator. It made five sandwiches. Thick and not so neat, the sandwiches used up space. And when I piled in a jar of pickles and two cans of peaches, an extra loaf of bread, all the onions there were for John, and two boxes of sweet crackers, the knapsack was stuffed. Without even room for the thermos. A jar of pickles went back, a can of peaches and a box of crackers.

I thought I was ruined, boiling up a pot of instant cocoa. I banged the pot. For five minutes I stood still as a chair in the dark kitchen. There wasn't any other sound. I boiled the cocoa and filled the thermos. And I was ready.

I ran the light around the kitchen for a last look. I noticed the door again with its four panels. I tiptoed upstairs to my bedroom for the scout knife I remembered about. It was in the top drawer of my dresser. I took a last look at the bedroom. I noticed the pennant my father gave me, over the bed, Massachusetts Institute of Technology. Onion John and I would take a walk past the Institute, someday, I thought, to see what it was like.

The numbers on my alarm clock were dim in the dark. It was eleven thirty. That gave me a half hour to get out to the piano factory. There was time to spare. And I didn't think so much of waiting around for Onion John in back of the piano factory, blowing the way it was outside and the curve growing in the corner of my window from the snow. But there was nothing to keep me any longer. Nothing more to do. And no reason why I shouldn't get started. This was one night I was going to be out in, anyway, for as long as it lasted. Ten minutes more wasn't going to make any difference.

I went down a step at a time. I felt carefully, one foot after another, on each stair before I let my weight go. One of them squeaks, depending on the weather. None did, this time. At least none of the upper stairs did. I never did get to find out about the last eight steps.

Because the front doorbell rang. I stood still in the dark that was turned into a boiler factory, with the doorbell ringing. The whole house shook, or I did, and shivered with the machine gun clang that came up. The light went on behind me and my father was at the top of the stairs with one arm in his bathrobe.

"Andy! What are you doing, up?" He came to where I was. "With your mackinaw on?" He didn't give me a chance to answer, rushing past to get to the doorbell ringing. I couldn't anyway, being choked. And I didn't have to answer my mother either when she showed up in her dressing gown. "Good grief!" She came down the steps. "Great heavens, Andy, look at you!" There was nothing you had to say to those remarks.

By that time my father had the door open.

And there stood Onion John. He stood with a heavy bag over his shoulder and he was embroidered in snow. Eechee had him fixed up fine. He had an army coat again, a long one. And a stocking cap, a blue one that came up to a ball instead of a point. There were heavy shoes on his feet, good ones for walking, and around his pants he'd wrapped a pair of puttees made out of burlap. He couldn't be dressed any better for a trip.

He stood in the door with the fingers of his left hand pinned together and he circled them, talking away.

My father wrung his head as if to get the water out of his ears. "What's this all about?" He turned to me. "What's he saying?"

"On account of it's a cold night, he thinks if you don't want to get the house chilled it would be better if he could close the door. That is, if you don't mind for him to come in to the hall." I got it out before my voice twisted up. I didn't have any more control over it than a busted radio.

My father didn't make me out too well, either. He squinted up the staircase. "And you?" he threw off another shake of the head. "What is this?"

"Yes, Andy," my mother had me tight around the shoulders, "what is this?"

"I don't know," I tuned myself down. "Whatever it is, I guess it's all off. Except Onion John wants to know can he come in?"

"Of course, John. Get in here!" My father pulled the

door wide. John dropped his bag. He unbuttoned his over-coat and ruffled it to get the snow off. Underneath he was wearing a nice tan raincoat that had a belt around it. It was a new looking raincoat so he was wearing it inside, I imagine, to protect it from the weather. He stamped his feet. And all the while he looked at me, serious, as if he couldn't wait to tell me what he had in mind.

I couldn't wait, either, watching him come in. Except my father kept piling him with questions. Where'd he been? What did he think he was doing? Didn't he realize the whole town was looking for him, with everybody worried? And my mother had another pile to ask me. How come I was all dressed up? Did I know what time of the night it was? And where was I going?

John stood at the foot of the staircase and I sat down. We stared at each other, waiting for the chance that my father and mother would get through. My father stopped first. Onion John told my father that he'd come to see me.

"Why?" I asked him. "Why did you have to call it off? You're not going back to fumigating, don't tell me that!"

John got as far as to say, no, he'd given that up. When my father came in again.

"If you'd only give him half a minute?" I asked my father.

"What's called off?" asked my mother.

"Andy, I want to know what goes on here?"

"I don't know. I mean it. If you'd only let me find out,·

I'd be glad to tell you. Just half a minute is all." My father held still. My mother sat down beside me. The three of us waited on Onion John. He came around the bottom of the staircase and he talked to me through the banisters.

He told me nothing was called off, as far as leaving Serenity went. That was still the idea.

"Except can't you see, John, it's wrecked. With you coming here! What was wrong with the piano factory? For Heaven's sakes, John, the way we planned."

"What plans?"

"Let them be, Andrew," said my mother.

Onion John told me, then, that he was going to leave Serenity without me. He told me that I couldn't go with him. He told me he sat up in McKardle's cave and that many hours went by with him looking at the fire. And after all that time, when he had nothing more to look at except red coals, he decided. He came to the place where he changed his mind about me. He decided he would run away alone. I couldn't come with him. He said he was sorry.

"What's the matter with me?" I asked him. "Why?"

Onion John told me I was grown up.

"What?" I looked over the rail at him. "What're you talking about?"

John nodded very slowly, like a principal in school. He was pretty sure, he said. He looked at it from every angle before he decided. And there wasn't any doubt in his mind what happened to me.

"Andy? What's the trouble?" asked my mother. With one finger under my chin, she closed my mouth.

My father came up the stairs and kneeled on the step below us. "What'd John say?"

"He said I was grown up."

My father and mother examined each other for a second, very surprised. "When did it happen?" asked my father.

"John says this afternoon."

"How does he know?"

John shrugged and told me he'd had enough experience. After twenty-five years in Serenity, he pointed out where he'd become an expert in small boys. They were the only ones he got along with when it came to doing things together. And the day always came, he noticed, with every one of them, when they stopped believing in him. When they just didn't see any more sense in the things he did. All through those twenty-five years in Serenity it happened over and over again. As one, then another, grew up.

And that afternoon, John nodded his head at me through the banisters, it happened to me.

"Good grief," I said. "When?"

"Foolish." John spoke the word clearer than that afternoon, as if he'd been rehearsing it. It was because of what I thought about that far-fetched idea he had, with the oak fire, how it would never work. That was it. That's why he changed his mind. If I didn't believe him anymore, how was it possible for us to get along together? We couldn't.

It was too late, John shook his head. I was too far gone to run away with.

"It just isn't so," I told him. I raised myself up a step. "I don't care how many angles you looked at." I lifted back another step. "It isn't, John, it just isn't so!"

"What isn't so?" My mother watched me climb the stairs backwards.

"I'm not grown up," I yelled at John through the posts. "The whole idea you had, it wasn't practical. It wouldn't ever work."

"What wouldn't?" asked my mother.

"Andy, can't you let us in on this?" My father followed me up a couple of steps.

"All right, John, you listen to my father. He'll tell you himself." I pointed to a flower in the stair carpet, just for something to point at. "If you got up tomorrow morning," I asked my father, "and you breathed some smoke from an oak fire, would that make any difference to you?"

"How, Andy? In what way?"

"Would it get rid of any of the evil spirits in you?"

"Evil who?" My father caught at the rail and straightened up. After a second, he passed the question along to my mother. "In me?"

She looked puzzled too. "Is that the way you think of your father, Andy? You think he's evil?"

"No, I'm not saying that." I pointed to the flower and made it clear for them. "Pa's great. There's no doubt about

211

it. He thinks only kind thoughts. And all he's out to do is what's best, for the best reasons, and the best arguments. Like he wants to build a new house to make John happy. And me. He wants me to go to the moon so I'll have the best career. It's only the way the thought works out. What happens to it. It don't make John happy. And me neither, not about General Magneto. The only one it makes happy is the evil spirit that's turned up in Pa. And all I'm asking—"

"Whoa, Andy! Hold it!" My father felt around with his knee and he shifted to sit down on the step where he was. "We can't take all that for granted! That there are evil spirits in me!"

"We don't have to. All it gets down to is this. Yes or no. Would an oak fire, the smell of it, stop you from building John's house again?"

I don't know why it took my father so long. His attention was caught by the carpet in front of him, by the design of it.

"It's a simple enough question."

"As far as it goes," my father sighed, "I guess it wouldn't stop me. No."

"There, did you hear that?" I yelled at John. I threw one leg over the rail and slid half way. I jumped the last four steps into the hall. "The whole idea of fumigating, John, it was useless. That's why I said foolish. It doesn't have anything to do with how old I am. Any baby in a cradle would tell you the same thing."

John acted like I had temperature. He smoothed my shoulder. It didn't make any difference, he said, the way my father agreed with me. It was only more proof, even, I was grown up. He pulled the top button of his overcoat closed.

"But, John!" I raised my hand. And I looked at it, at my hand. What was it doing up there? What was the point of arguing? Even if I convinced Onion John I was the same as always, I couldn't walk out of the house past my father and mother and go along with him. "Can't you see," I let my hand down, " how things are?"

John closed his eyes to show how sorry he was for me. Never in his life, he said, had he heard of anyone who was in more trouble than I. But there was nothing he could do about it. And now it was time he got started.

"Not tonight!" I walked backwards, ahead of him down the hall. He had to give me another chance. He had to wait until we could get off somewhere, just the two of us and we could talk. So I could get him to understand we were still good friends and nothing was changed. "Please!"

The way he went about it was very gentle. There wasn't any push to it, or shove. But I was like a stranger he met who was blocking the sidewalk. He took me by the shoulders and he set me over to one side, out of his way. It was as if we were passing by somewhere, the way he acted, and he was going one way and me another.

"Where's he going?" asked my mother.

For the life of me I couldn't see what I'd done, so wrong, for us to end up strangers this way.

"Andy?"

"I don't know where he's going. Except he's running away from Serenity, by himself."

"By himself? You mean that's what you were up to, Andy?" My mother was right behind. She pulled me around. "Andy, you were running away from home?"

She looked even more beautiful than at supper because her face, the color of it, was like she'd been walking through the wind.

"Not anymore," I told her. "I'm too old for it. That's what John says."

My mother took the black and white hunting hat off my head and held it to her dressing gown. "Onion John, I don't know how to thank you for coming here tonight."

"That was very wise and helpful of you, John. Once a boy grows up, you're right, he can't run away from home. That's no way for him to get anywhere!" My father put a hand on John's arm, to keep him from buttoning his overcoat. "And you can't either. You can't run away from Serenity. Your home's here. We're your friends. We want to help you."

John shook his head. "That sounds like another lie," I told my father.

"Another what?" The fists my father made, he put into the pockets of his bathrobe.

"It's something like what I told John this afternoon. I said I wanted to help him. Then I saw I was trying to work things out for myself. More than to help just him. It was too big a lie for me to handle. I don't know about you. Anyway, John says he can't use any more help."

John nodded to show that's the way he felt about it. He finished with his overcoat and went to work on the big collar it had, tucking himself in. Which was just as well, from the noise the wind made in the quiet of the hall.

"John," my father's hands were open again. "I won't ask you to believe me. But one thing you can see is true, beyond question. You can help us. The town. It's not only how ridiculous we'll feel, if you leave. Though that's part of it, to be honest with you. We're proud of what we tried to do. And it will be a blow, to our self-respect, if you throw it all back at us and walk out. John, would you listen to me?"

It was a tough collar to close. John was bent half backwards, looking at the ceiling, trying to get the loop over a button. With his elbows out, stiff, he looked to be strangling himself.

"It won't do you any good, asking John for his help." I didn't want to see my father go to all that trouble. "I asked him too. He just won't."

My father went to John's rescue and the two of them got the collar, at least, straightened out.

"But it isn't only our pride, John, that's not why I'm

216

asking you to help. It's a great deal more important than pride. If you leave Serenity, the people here will be shy of every kind hearted thought that comes along. The next time there's a real need, no matter what, we'll hesitate. We'll get suspicious of ourselves. On account of what's happened to you. If you leave, John, you'll leave this town cold. And scared to make even the smallest move that's friendly. That's why you have to stay and help us."

John listened, now he was dressed snug, till my father finished. Then he put his hands to his chest and he shrugged. He explained how he felt.

"He won't stay?" asked my father.

"He can't help. He's tried. Up at the house he tried his best to do everything you wanted. He can't manage it. And he's not going to try anymore."

"And the rest? What else was he saying?"

"Nothing. Except if he could help anyone, he would like to help me."

"What else, Andy?"

"Well, it's only his way of talking."

"Tell me."

"Well, he said he never heard of any father who would send his only son to the moon. He heard of kings putting their boy on top of a castle. Or in a cave with a dragon outside. But I was the first he ever came across, getting shipped to the moon. And he was interested to help me, if he could. The only chance though, he thinks, is fumigating."

"Good night!" My father rubbed his eyes, tired as he was, considering the time and all his hard talking. "Doesn't he know how foolish that is?"

"Well, I did try to tell him that."

"So you did." My father's smile, when he took his hand away from his mouth, was tired too. "I never thought," he said to my mother, "we'd ever hear Andy call an idea of Onion John's foolish. If nothing else comes out of this, I think maybe your son has grown up."

He pulled the cord of his bathrobe tighter. His arms crossed and he held on to his elbows, but this time it was like he was holding himself together in front of Onion John. "All right, John. Maybe I am filled with evil spirits. And maybe we did try to lie to you, Andy and I. But all that's over with. You win."

What was win? John wanted to know.

"We're going to forget the house. We'll call it off. At the meeting tomorrow night. Let Ernie Miller get up on his hind legs and crow. But there won't be any new house, Onion John. We'll vote it down."

Onion John had his head twisted, listening with his right ear. "My father's trying to tell you," I went to him, "you don't have to run away. It's going to be the way you want. No house. You can stay here in Serenity."

Onion John stood there in our hall, buttoned up in his overcoats, and along with the wind piling around the corner outside, my father and mother and I listened to Onion John.

He thought the best thing he could do was leave. He was going.

"But I promise you," said my father. "We'll vote it down. Believe me."

Onion John told me what to say. "He believes you. But votes, he doesn't know so much about them. The good they are for getting people cleaned up. This week's vote is No, could be, and next week it turns out to be Yes. You never know. And besides, votes only go so far."

"Yes, Andy?"

"He mentioned, you vote about a house and that's as far as it goes."

"What else is there?"

"He sees where lots of different things can happen and there's no vote to them."

"Like what, Andy? Do we have to pull teeth?"

"What he had in mind, was the moon. How's a vote, he wants to know, going to keep anyone from being shipped to the moon."

"Andy! Tell him, Andy, can't you get him to see we're talking about him. Only him. You're no part of this anymore. You're grown up. Whatever concerns you, that's your affair and it's for you to decide, for yourself."

"Me?" That hall was no place for anyone wearing a mackinaw. It was warm. I took the time to pull down my zipper. "I'm the one to decide? Even about General Magneto?"

"Yes." My mother slipped the coat off and she held it. "That's what your father means." And my father said exactly the same thing. "Yes. That's right."

What I probably did was, I sat down. Anyway there I was on the bottom step looking up at them. I don't know what the three of them expected, watching me so close. Maybe that I'd dash upstairs for the bathroom, now I was grown up, to start shaving. John gave me a nice smile, as long as everybody agreed with him how much I'd aged. He turned slowly and started for the door.

I jumped for him and I grabbed him. "Not now, Onion John! Why? Nothing's going to happen to you. Or to me either. It's all going to be the same. If you'll only stick around, the same as always."

Still smiling John picked me off from his left arm where I had a hammer lock, like I was a bramble he was caught in.

"Please," said my mother. "There's an extra bed. In this storm, it's a terrible night for running away."

"Don't leave Serenity?" asked my father.

Onion John spread the fingers of one hand to wipe down his mustache. They went on to circle his chin. He talked slowly.

"He says he's got to go except—the only way he could ever stay in Serenity," I told my father and mother, "is to fumigate. To burn an oak fire up at McKardle's cave. If it ever worked, there wouldn't have to be any votes. The town

220

would be swept clean again and tidy. No one would have to be afraid of any nice thoughts or good feelings. But he doesn't suppose it's very practical from all we tell him. And he'd like to ask us just once more. Do we honestly think there's no use to it at all?"

I waited for my father to answer first. He thought it over and he said, "I'm afraid not." Even if it would keep Onion John in Serenity, it was too much for me to handle to say anything else but, "No." My mother said, "No, John, I don't think so." Onion John nodded as if he hadn't heard anything other than what he expected, and he might as well be on his way.

A couple of snowflakes whirled in, when the door opened, and they slowed to settle down and disappear. Ours is a big deep porch so it had to be snowing heavy and blowing hard for snowflakes to carry across. Once the door went wide you could see how heavy and hard the storm was. In the small light of the street lamp outside, it looked as if Serenity was filled with smoke. Until another gust hit, like the muffled crack of a wave breaking, and the wind carried the snow into a steady slant. There was a drift against the burlap bag as it lay on the porch. The pile broke and the snow scattered off the bag as it swung to John's shoulder.

Onion John stood in the light of the door and he smiled to the three of us in the hall. He felt on the top of his hat. "Well, good day," he lifted the little ball. The door closed and Onion John was gone.

Chapter 18

It was hard to believe. It was something awful and it was wonderful, there were two sides to what happened. And both were hard to believe.

When the shovels starting scraping the next morning and I went to the window for a look at the Rorty's down the street, where Onion John is always the first one shoveling snow, I remembered the worse part. He was gone.

And when I went back to reach under the bed for my socks, I remembered the wonderful part that was left. How I was still in Serenity and the only one it was up to for next summer and always, was me.

It seemed too good to be true, what happened, and too bad.

I went to find my father and he was down in the cellar stoking up the furnace before breakfast. I checked both sides of how things stood. There wasn't any doubt about Onion John. My father only hoped John didn't have to wait too long, heavy as the storm had been all night, until he got a hitch. My father closed the furnace door and looked around where he left the snow shovel way back last spring, so we could clean off the walks before we went up to eat. It was then I asked about the good part, whether he really meant what he said about me the night before.

My father found the snow shovel and he handed it to me. It was the same as an answer. I always get the coal shovel when we dig out after a storm. It's smaller. When he gave me the big one, it meant there wasn't any doubt that I was grown up.

"And I'm the one to decide about myself?" I was halfway down the driveway, right behind him, cutting a narrow path alongside the house.

He said, "Yes," same as the night before.

"Well, I've decided," I told him when we reached the sidewalk out front.

"No, you haven't." He heaved the shovelful he had and turned around. "You haven't had time to think about it."

"All the way out here," I told him. "I've had the last ten, twelve minutes to think about it."

"It's the rest of your life you're deciding on. Don't you figure you ought to give it a little more time?"

"That's so!" I leaned on my shovel. "I suppose I ought."

I gave it until afternoon, when I could get down to the hardware store. Even though in between, I didn't have much time to myself for thinking, the shock there was at school that Onion John had run away from Serenity. The

223

only one not shocked was Eech. And he was surprised that I was still around. When I described how I could stay in Serenity now, I got a promise from Eech. Not to mention about McKardle's cave. Everyone was asking, why? Why did Onion John leave town? I didn't especially want them to know it was on account of me, because I told him he shouldn't fumigate.

When I did show up at the hardware store there was a gang, men, and they were discussing Onion John, too. I asked my father if he wouldn't mind stepping over to the desk, away from the others.

"I've decided," I told him, "about General Magneto next summer and M.I.T. and, you know, going to the moon. What I want to do the rest of my life. And I think the best thing—"

"No, Andy. Hold it." He lifted me up and sat me on the desk. "I don't want to hear your decision, not yet. Not until you've really considered it. Thought it through."

"I've had all day."

"It's the most important decision you'll ever make. Give it time."

"Until tomorrow?"

"Give it months. Years, even."

What was the use of being the one who was going to decide if it took that long? "Why wait? You were the one, I thought you wanted to get it settled so quick."

"I know. Maybe that was a very big mistake."

"I don't see any mistake to it. Wouldn't it be better if we knew how things stood? What's the use for such a long time?"

"Look, Andy." My father slammed the carriage of the typewriter and the bell went. "We're trying to figure out if there's anything we can do about Onion John. There's the meeting tonight. No one really believes Onion John's gone for good. The least we can do is fix things so he'll want to come back. Let's see what happens to Onion John first."

"Before I tell you my decision? But that could be as long as what you said, months or years. He may never come back."

"On the other hand," my father nodded over to the men, "a lot of them believe he'll be coming back in a day or so. Mr. Donahue does, and Herm Ries. Anyway, for the fish drive. He hasn't missed one of those in twenty years. They're sure he'll be back for that. Let's wait, at least until the fish drive."

"All right. I'll tell you what I decide, then."

The fish drive could come along almost any time. It didn't depend on the calendar, only on the weather. When it turned cold enough. The fish drive was always the first Saturday after the Musconetty froze over. That couldn't be very long, the early winter we were having. And if the hunch Donahue had was right, or Mr. Ries, Onion John might be back even before. And then there wouldn't be any more bad to what happened, it would all be good.

I certainly hoped everybody was right, the way they looked for Onion John to come walking along Route 96, some morning, with that burlap bag over his shoulder.

To listen to them all, you'd think they were talking about the courthouse. Onion John could no more disappear out of Serenity, everybody agreed, than the courthouse could get up and wander off into the night. One was as much a fixed and regular part of town as the other. And everybody had a different part to remember about Onion John, that only he knew about.

It could be only the nickel John gave them when they were six. Or the way he showed them how to spit on bait to make it better for eels. Or the figure he drew, maybe, on a kite to make it fly higher. Or no more than a walk they took with him along toward dark, through the wind and past the shadows when Onion John scared them with the noises he made and then got them to laughing with the faces he put on. Each one had something to recall, whenever they saw Onion John, about long ago. Something good they might forget, now he wasn't around to remind them.

So they all asked, why? Why did he ever take it into his head he had to leave Serenity at all, much less for good? That was the big question at the council meeting that night.

If Onion John was so hard rock set against the house, everyone argued, that didn't mean he had to run away. It was easy enough getting rid of the house. All anyone had to do about that was raise their hand, when the time came.

And that's what did happen that night. After my father let Ernie Miller get up on the platform and roam around for a half an hour, going into politics and democracy and whatever, all my father had to do was get up and say he agreed with Ernie, one hundred percent. And with just a couple of words, he made a bigger fuss at the meeting than Ernie did with his whole speech.

When my father announced that Serenity was wrong, the way it went at Onion John, and the worst one wrong was himself, there wasn't any argument. The assembly hall at the courthouse looked like a field of sprouting corn when the vote was called. It was against the new house, building it for Onion John when he came back.

Except the vote didn't answer anyone's main question, why did he have to run away at all? We were the only ones who knew, my father and I, the whole reason.

"Do you think we have to tell them?"

"Tell them what?" My father went ahead of me through the paths on the sidewalk, on the way home from the meeting.

"Why Onion John left." Walking on the dry stiff snow, my father squeaked out ahead like a cork in a bottle. "I'd hate for everyone to know it was because of you and me. Because we told him an oak fire was senseless and that's why he left."

My father pulled up for a drifted stretch and I bumped into him. He turned. "Is that the reason?"

"It was on account of us, wasn't it?"

"It was on account of us, all right!" My father took into the deep snow and plowed through in his galoshes. "And I guess we'll have to admit it. Unless we're lucky and he does come back." He pounded the snow off his feet. "How about if we wait, Andy, before we tell anybody why Onion John left. Anyway, until the fish drive."

There was a lot getting hung up on that fish drive to wait for. It's a thing that goes on every year and it's been going on for a long time, the last hundred years or so. Soon as the ice gets thick enough on the Musconetty, a crowd shows up to drive fish. What happens is, there's a net gets sunk across the creek and then a mob of maybe eighty or ninety back off about a half a mile and chase the fish, whooping and banging on the ice, downstream into the net.

The fish drive doesn't happen on schedule. There's never any announcement about it, any posters in the window like for a covered dish supper at the Methodists, or any committees to organize what's coming. It happens naturally. When the temperature goes down close to zero and hangs down there for three or four days, in the still hard cold that's come, you naturally get ready for next Saturday.

And even though there isn't any plan to it, or very much talk, everyone you expect shows up early that morning somewhere below Conroy's Bend fattened out in their extra sweaters and mufflers and overshoes and gloves. Each one brings his own lunch and his own tools for chopping and

228

banging. Farmer Dusek brings the net, a special one made out of Irish linen with two inch mesh. It's about twelve feet deep and sixty feet wide, enough to reach across the creek from bank to bank. Marty Bemeth brings a chain saw. He uses it to cut a path across the creek, a stretch of open water three feet wide. On the downstream side of this cut, the net is hung on a half dozen posts that stand on the bed of the stream. It blocks the creek from shore to shore.

Everything about a fish drive happens in a set and natural way. A fire starts up near the net and everyone stands around it, before they get going, to have a last drink out of what they brought for lunch, of something hot. Or the first drink, for some of the men, of hard cider or applejack. You need bolstering up inside, cold as it always is.

Then one or two wander off upstream and pretty soon we're all on our way, taking down saplings for clubs or cutting branches as we go. There's usually a wait at the place the drive commences until everyone collects. And then someone flips his cigarette and says, "Well," and the first wave takes off.

These are the choppers. There's ten or twelve of them with axes and they go downstream in a line, cutting holes across the creek about two yards apart every twenty feet or so. After them come the stirrers who carry long poles to put down through the holes to stir up a commotion that will get the fish moving. And then come all the rest of us, we're the beaters, with axes and clubs and sledgehammers, jumping and yelling and banging, to chase the stirred up fish downstream ahead of us.

There's plenty of noise to it, even when the first line of choppers move out. And by the time the beaters join in, the whole winding silvery creek sounds like Serenity was going over for one long continuous touchdown. Cold as it is, the morning's right for jumping and yelling as well as, for some of the men, more hard cider and applejack. To the fish below, it must sound like the world's come to an end.

And for about fifteen hundred pounds of them, the world does come to an end, their world at least. We usually haul six to eight hundred fish, averaging two pounds apiece. It takes a lot of weight and muscle to pull in the ropes that roll the net over that dark and wriggling catch from down below.

Most of them are suckers. There oughtn't to be any trout or bass because the season on those fish is closed. That's the reason we use such a big mesh, two inches, to let the game fish through. But if the trout and the others are so big they get caught anyway, then every year we decide it's their fault, not ours, and we divide them up with the rest. A trout or a bass isn't any better, really, than a midwinter sucker. Summers, a sucker that you take out of water that's warm and muddy isn't worth the trouble. But in the winter, a sucker is firm and clean as any fish you'd want on your table.

The fish get divided up while we eat. Lunch takes a long time because of all the food everyone brings and all the hard cider there is, for some of the men, and applejack. And because there's a lot to talk over about the fish drive that's finished and the fish dinner that's coming.

For the sport it is, a lot of people judge the fish drive to be the best thing that happens in Serenity every year. Onion John thought so. He was the most important man to show up for a fish drive.

Because even though no one's in charge, there's always one second when someone has to say, "Now!" When to haul in the net. The exact second has to be figured to the hair. It can't be too soon, before the fish are all crowded in. And it can't be too late, after the beaters come too close, because they'll drive the fish back from the net, upstream. "Now!" —the time to lay hold of the net—has to be said just right.

And somehow, Onion John never missed. He'd stand there on the ice with his head cocked and his eyes closed and his hand up. You'd think he had some way of knowing what went on in the deep dark, below. The message would come and his hand would drop, some years early and some years "Now!" came long after anyone thought was right. But year after year the haul we'd get with Onion John was always half again better, according to some of the older men, than the fish they caught before John showed up.

It was only natural, Onion John never missed a fish drive. And that's why everyone was sure he'd be coming back to Serenity, at the very latest, for the one this year.

But when the temperature went to six degrees of cold right before Christmas, and the next day it held and the next one and the one after that stayed steely and bitter and hard to breathe, and when for two nights after it dipped to eight below zero until a row of white wicked teeth stretched across the falls on High Street and the Musconetty was ten inches solid with ice and when Saturday morning came and the fish drive and we waited for Onion John, he never showed up. And then we knew, hard as it was to believe, that he was gone from Serenity for good.

Chapter 19

We did it."

"What?" I asked my father.

"I'm afraid we've chased Onion John out of Serenity. He's disappeared."

"He might still be coming. And got held up. In traffic maybe."

My father shook his head. He dropped the edge of his axe, a four pound Widgecomb, down to the ice. He was dressed in his navy pea jacket and a heavy blue muffler and a blue hunting cap, too, all dark. It could've been church he was ready for, or someone coming to dinner and not for a fish drive.

We stood with about a hundred others down from the bridge across the Musconetty, where the road leaves Route 96 to go up to Hessian Hill. The crowd of us stood around and waited like the stretch of creek we were on was a depot, and there was a train coming. Now and then, there'd be someone who'd have another cigarette or more coffee or whatever it was they brought along. You didn't hear much talk. You saw it instead, little clouds that went from one to the other. In the quiet and in the cold we didn't move much as the time went and the sun came through the solid sky to spread a net of shadows on the Musconetty where we were bunched. In the trees along the creek there were lights the sun made, along the branches hung with snow, points that came on and went out.

"Traffic, maybe. Or else trouble getting a hitch."

"He's not coming," said my father.

"Let's face it," said someone on the other side of the crowd, "Onion John's not going to get here. How about moving?"

But there wasn't any answer and, instead, a couple of men lighted up to have one more cigarette and they stood still as chimneys with the smoke coming out along with the fog.

"You don't think there's any more chance at all?" I asked my father.

"I'm afraid not."

"And the time's come when we got to admit why he left?"

"At least to ourselves."

"And not tell the others?"

"I suppose so, Andy. I guess we should." My father didn't seem too anxious. I wasn't either. Except it was one of the things we promised to do when the fish drive came.

"Unless we have to make an announcement about it, I figured another way." I slipped the knapsack with our lunch off my back. "If I tell Ries and let him go, it'll be all over the place in ten or fifteen minutes. That might be a lot better than an announcement, less fuss."

"Go ahead." My father nodded. "Your way."

"Eechee Ries!" I yelled. He came over carrying a piece of locust he was going to use for a club. "You don't have to keep it a secret anymore, why Onion John left."

"Why did he?"

"Don't you remember? When I told him it was no use fumigating. That's why. And my father was in it too. He said the same thing. It was because of us."

"I see," said Eech. "What do you want me to do about it?"

"Do? Anything you feel like doing. I just want to let you out of the secret."

Eech didn't act as if it were too big a secret to tell about. He stopped to make a remark to George Connors. If anyone, Connors would be interested in news about me that was bad. He took a look over to where we stood, me and my father, but that's all. Watching Ries walk back into the crowd it didn't seem anyone was too interested in why Onion John left, anymore. Now they knew he was gone for good.

But at least I kept one of the promises we made for the fish drive, the hard one.

The talk came up louder. "Let's go!" And, "What's the use?" And, "This is it! He's gone." And, "What are we waiting for?" Cigarettes got tossed and axes and clubs picked up. And without any signal, the choppers walked out in a line.

The only noise was the crack and splinter of the ice as they drove the first string of holes across the creek. Without any more to do, the stirrers moved off and they stood, legs apart, across the Musconetty and worked the long poles quietly back and forth, around and around, in the water below. There was a lot more noise, naturally, when all the rest followed, as beaters. But it didn't sound like sport. Most of the noise was clubbing and hammering on the ice, without too much whooping and hollering.

I hung back. My father took a heavy swing and pounded the ice once.

That's when I asked him, "How about the other promise? Is it time?"

He straightened up and looked back at me.

"Do you want to hear now, what I've decided. About General Magneto and Technology? Or does that come later?"

"If you don't mind, I'd like to hear about that later."

"After the drive?"

"Much, much later. After we've had a chance to forget about this drive."

"But all you said we had to wait for was today!"

236

"I know." That one swing of a four pound axe, it looked, had made my father tired. "I was counting on Onion John I guess, to show up. You were never in such a hurry to make up your mind, when he was around."

"But he's gone. And you said today."

"I said it was up to you, Andy. And it is. Any decision that's made, you're the one that's going to make it. Isn't that enough, for the moment. Can't you wait?"

"I suppose I could. But I don't know how fair it is. After we talked it over, it was going to be today. Myself, I thought you'd want to hear. I always thought you wanted to get things settled, without wasting any time."

"I've told you, that was a mistake. A big one. I don't want you to make the same kind of mistake. To be in such a hurry."

"It isn't fair, though."

"Maybe not." My father looked at the blade of his axe and tested it with his thumb. "I think you ought to know, Andy." He stopped and forgot his axe. He watched the beaters hammering their way downstream. We were left behind. The two of us stood out on the ice alone in the middle of the creek. He turned back to me. "What I think you ought to know is, I'd like another cup of cocoa."

He picked up my knapsack and he went in to shore. He sat down in the overstuffed bankful of snow as if he'd just come in from a day at the store and was settling to have a look at the *Lamp*. He forced his elbows back, to get a stretch into his shoulders and then rummaged around in the knapsack to find the thermos. It had two cups on top, nested together, and he poured one to hold out to me. The steam of it floated away from his hand.

I didn't feel so much like cocoa, not with everything so undecided and getting hung up until who knows when. But it seemed like such a good idea to my father, the way he held the cup out, I took a couple of steps and slid into shore. The bank was soft as a sofa and the cup felt as if you were holding your hands out to a stove. You could trail the cocoa all the way down inside, the heat of it. My father's voice was quiet.

"What I think you ought to know about your father is this. He's nothing but a hardware storekeeper in a small town in New Jersey."

That's all he said, looking over the top of his cup, out across the ice. It sounded very important, the way he put it.

"What's there I ought to know, I mean about that?"

"Only that he wanted to be an engineer, somewhere else."

"Well, I do. I do know about that."

He leaned back and took a drink of cocoa. "How?"

"Mom told me."

"I see. Then that makes it a lot easier. As long as you know, I don't have to go into it, the kind of a failure I am. Or was, until you started coming along. And I thought I'd get there yet, up to M.I.T. and out into the world where the big things happen—I thought I'd get there yet through you." He looked into his cup. "That sounds pretty bad, doesn't it? Using you to make up for how I lost out. Like one of John's evil spirits who helps the next fellow so he can get what he wants for himself. But the worst of it—" He finished off his cocoa and swept what was left out across the ice, a circle of brown splotches and dots. "The worst, was how I wanted to be sure. How anxious I was to get you started. The hurry I was in. Someone was bound to get run over in the rush. And that's why I say, now, I think we ought to slow down a bit and wait, take it easy. Before anyone else gets hurt."

"Anyone else?"

My father looked around as if he was surprised I was still there, sitting next to him on the bank.

"Besides Onion John! We have to admit that we wrecked him bad enough. Once you took off to hide behind him, once I came chasing after you, before we got finished, well, not even Dick Ries thought it was much of a secret any more, why Onion John disappeared."

"No."

I handed my father the empty cup. He twisted it back on top of the thermos along with his own.

"So let's wait, Andy, before we make any big decisions. Don't you make the same mistake I did. There's school. And all the rest that goes on around town. If you keep up in your studies, all of them, when the time comes you can go whichever way you want. But for a while, forget you're grown up."

"How can I? It's happened."

"Well, then, get used to it. See how it feels before you decide what kind of grownup to be."

My father threw the thermos into the knapsack, only he missed. He caught the bottle before it slid too far and then he packed it carefully away.

"Let's get started. This is no way to spend the morning, sitting in the snow here and talking about mistakes and about failures. And all you've got to tell me, all it would amount to is one more failure. The point is, Andy, I don't want to hear what you have to tell me. Please, let it wait."

The only other time I ever heard my father want a favor so bad was in the hall, that night, with Onion John when there was nothing I could do about it.

"I'll wait," I told him. "Until whenever you want to hear about what I decide."

"Thanks." He shoved the knapsack over to me so I'd put it on. He picked up his axe. As if it were all over and there was nothing left except to catch up with the others. They were far downstream, near a bend, where a lot of sunlight came through to the ice. There was plenty of yelling by now. It sounded more like a fish drive. I expected by this time of the morning when the fish drive came, I'd have everything said to my father so he'd know what I had in mind. And I'd know what he thought about it.

"It's only I'd like to tell you how I've been turning things over. Not a decision about anything. Just the general idea I have."

"Don't you think we ought to get going?"

I started to buckle up the knapsack. "Just another half minute."

The *Lamp* was stuck in the outside pocket where I'd put it the night I was going to run away. It reminded me of when it was hot and it was noontime back in August and I asked my father about the ball club picture, "Who am I?" I should've stopped when he answered me and then none of this would have happened. When he told me to look from left to right and I saw I was "Andrew J. Rusch, Jr." My father was right, then, and that's what I told him now.

"I'm the same as you. The same name and all. And I'd just as soon go on being you, as much as anyone I've ever met. I'm not talking about Woodrow Wilson and those, who are supposed to be great. I'm saying the only one I ever come across, who's anything great, is you. It was along those lines what I had in mind."

He stopped from getting up at least. He eased back into the snow and the axe dropped, so it rested on the ice between his knees. He seemed comfortable enough, watching a boulder across the way that was coated up and shining in the sun. As long as he didn't mind listening, I thought I'd get a little more in.

"I don't know about General Magneto, if there's any one

great down there. Maybe there is, but why waste a whole summer looking around. Because it's not a question of failure. I don't see how you can say that. The thing is if you were an engineer, well, that's what I'd like to be. And if you were going to the moon, I'd go there. But as long as you're in the hardware business, all I'm trying to say is I don't want to be anything special in particular. Except you. Seeing the start I have in that direction anyway. And what I thought." He seemed to be resting easy. "If you don't mind just another second?"

"Go ahead."

"Not that it's any decision. I'll wait about that. But just as a matter of judgment I thought the best thing I could do was to look over the possibilities in Serenity, down with you at the hardware store. That seems sensible."

Walking a fence wasn't any worse than showing my father what I had in mind without saying it right out, positively. I don't know whether I went too far before I quit.

When I did it was quiet. The racket from the fish drive below was a faraway noise you couldn't tell about, whether it was yelling or traffic or trees in a storm. A breeze did come from downstream and the snow shook off the branches like it was a celebration, and it was confetti coming down. Except there was nothing to celebrate until I heard my father's opinion about what I mentioned. I couldn't see anything in that boulder he was looking at, worth all the time he gave it.

"You don't mind I went into it so far?"

"I don't mind."

We sat and got nowhere. After a while my father put his hands behind his head and leaned back till you'd think he was in his reading chair at home, with his feet stretched out. The boulder across the way must have turned into a shape, the way a rock does when you stare at it, like a face or an animal. My father smiled at whatever he saw.

"After all, it's not as if you've arrived at any decision."

"No. I promised you about that."

"Well, just as a general point of view I'd say it was about as interesting as anything I've heard for a long time, in years."

"You don't see anything wrong about it?"

"I wouldn't go so far as to say whether it was right or wrong, Andy. But interesting, there's no question."

"So that, you could almost say you agree with me. That it's all right."

"Better than that. It's like the time we went out for pheasant with Onion John. I don't know if I agree with him to this day, about what happened. But it was wonderful, wasn't it?"

"I remember."

"It's like that here, this morning, with you."

The position he was in, bent way over backwards, seemed all right for smiling. But when it came to laughing, my father had to sit up. It wasn't a big laugh, the kind there is after a joke. It was a deep one, covered up, and the only part to see was what escaped. This was everything I'd ever waited until the fish drive for. I'd said what I had in mind, most of it. My father listened. He did better than agree with me. He laughed.

"But don't forget," he leaned on his knees. "This is not your final decision."

"Certainly not."

"Promise me one thing, Andy. In the next two or three years you'll be hearing a lot of new things. There'll be a good deal to learn and to see you never knew existed. Promise me you'll keep an open mind, whatever you run into. So that when the time does come to decide, you might want to change it, change your mind."

"Is that what you want?"

"Frankly, that's what I want."

"That I should change my mind about you?"

"No!" It was a shout, a loud one.

He looked at me sideways. He shook his head in a slant. "No, I'm not saying that."

His look slid away and went out over the creek. He saw where there was a knob of ice, almost a mushroom, about five feet out. He got up to go over to that. He kicked it, one boot that broke it into chips, slithering across the ice.

"All I'm saying is, when the time comes you make up your own mind."

"You said that."

"I guess I did. I guess the truth is, there's nothing more I can say."

My father held up my knapsack like a coat. I slipped into it. He picked up his axe. There was a hemlock branch I'd cut for a club, and it lay out on the ice. I picked it up and we took off, me and my father, to catch up with the others far down the creek.

I thought I knew what a great day was. It had to be a day with a band in it some place and a majorette out front lifting her knees. Crowds had to be a part of it, waving over each other's heads and applauding at the same time. And cheering, plenty of that, with yell leaders out front wearing tight sweaters they had to pull down. And a speech where every fifth word was your own name. And getting punched and shoved and pounded on the back until you ached. And laughing, everyone bent over. That was my idea.

But this was a great day. The greatest, for me, yet. It was nothing like what I thought. All we did was to walk down the Musconetty, slicked over with a shine across it.

Far from any bands, they would've been out of place. The creek was more like a long church, with the frosted trees arched over and the branches tangled so you'd think of windows with pictures in them that you see in church. The cheering and yelling there was from the fish drive was too far off, now, to amount to more than a quiet, heavy beat. It could've been a choir going through a low part.

There weren't any speeches. Or even talk. My father didn't have anything more to say. And neither did I. We understood what each of us wanted the other to know.

There wasn't any laughing. Except once when my father pulled up for a couple of seconds and he looked overhead, to laugh at nothing in particular.

We did a good deal of smiling when we happened to turn to each other. Which is the least you'd expect, considering the great day it turned out to be.

There was, though, a good deal of pounding. It began with my father when we came up to the first big bend. I thought he was struck with a thought when he stopped. But he let heave a full circle swing with his axe and he brought it, hammer side down, on the ice. The creek boomed and a crack snaked across stream.

I tried the best I could for an answer. But a hemlock branch can't compare to a four pound Widgecomb axe, not to mention my heft when compared to my father. The place I clubbed was near a stirring hole and the water jumped. At least, it was a different kind of an effect. Good enough for my father to let go again and answer me. And I answered him. We took to pounding, first him then me, and that's the way we went around the bend. It was one way to let off steam and useful for getting a move into any fish that were left behind, stragglers.

Just before we took the last of the bend, I looked back to where we'd been sitting.

You could see the spot from the way the snow was bunched, where we shoved back into it. It had the shape we were, the head and shoulders. Mine anyway. My father's was hid behind a tree. I remembered the song of Onion John's, the one he sang on Halloween, because this sight was something like in the song. Where the fellow goes floating down the river and he sees himself getting left behind on the bank. And he hears goodbye. Or the way Onion John would say it, farewell.

One step further and I couldn't see the shape, anymore. It was around the bend.

The End

Chapter 20

Two minutes after Andrew J. Rusch, Jr. and his father turned the bend of Musconetty Creek, a thin column of smoke rose above the hill west of Serenity where Mc-Kardle's cave is located. The prevailing breeze was from the west and the smoke drifted toward the town. From the smell of the smoke, it was an oak fire that was burning.

J. K.